Beat
Until Stiff

Beat
Until Stiff

Claire M. Johnson

Poisoned Pen Press

Poisoned Pen Press
6962 E. First Ave., Ste. 103
Scottsdale, AZ 85251
www.poisonedpenpress.com
info@poisonedpenpress.com

Printed in the United States of America

To my father, Gordon Henry Johnson

Acknowledgments

First of all, I must thank my family: my husband, Mark, who for the past three years has yet to finish a mystery novel without saying, "Your book is a thousand times better"; my children, Emma and Paul, who have been robbed of Thursday nights with Mom for the last four years as I drive off to my critique group, hell or high water; my parents, Martha and Ken Horne, at whose kitchen table we were expected to have something intelligent to say and were given the chance to say it; my sister, Valerie Mighetto, someone with a heart as big as the Ritz; and, finally, my in-laws, John and Luanne Sarconi. If they hadn't generously loaned me the money to finish up at the Culinary Academy, I'd never have had the material to write this book.

I attended a reading and discussion by a well-known, extremely successful writer who decried critique groups, saying they were destructive. I disagree. I would not be published today if it weren't for my Thursday night critique group. I tweaked and re-tweaked this book in response to their comments, and I consider them co-authors: Kay Barnhart, Mike Cooper, Janet Finsilver, Rena Leith, Ann Parker, Carole Price, and Gordon Yano. I would especially like to thank Kay. She and I met over four years ago at a California Writers' Club luncheon and read the truly horrible first draft. And the little less awful, but still bad, second draft, and the third, etc. Thanks, Partner in Crime.

Two people in the mystery world deserve special thanks: Camille Minichino and Penny Warner. Both of them invited me into their homes for writing classes, and this book never would have been published without their expertise. Penny deserves special thanks. Her confidence in my book was extremely important while I languished in unpublished hell, giving me the extra push to try yet one more publisher.

This book is primarily about the food industry, with a little mystery thrown in for flavor. The professional food world is a little like the writing world; it attracts the slightly off-kilter, the creative, the restless mind. One person I'd like to mention is Chef Leo Koellner, my teacher at the California Culinary Academy. A true professional who harbored none of the sexism so prevalent when I first started in the profession, it is because of mentors like him that the most exciting chefs in the United States today are women.

Finally, I would like to thank Robert Rosenwald and Barbara Peters, the gods behind Poisoned Pen Press. I'd about given up hope. Thanks for seeing what I see in this book. I especially thank Barbara for NOT living up to her reputation as the Evil Editor.

Chapter 1

I debated whether it would be worth ten years in San Quentin if I beat Thom to death with the salt and pepper shakers.

He continued to complain, cajole, bitch, beg, mope, and wheedle—we'd only been seated for five minutes.

"So she changed her mind. What's the big deal? Those chocolate owls," he snorted in derision. Thom's manicured nails alit on a bottle of that five dollars-a-liter Italian mineral water he favors. He took several tiny sips before continuing. "Mrs. Gerson wants something literary. It's a benefit for the new library. Be creative, for God's sake. Think *theme*."

My name is Mary Ryan. I'm cranky, recently divorced, and thirty-four years old. I'd been on my feet since five that morning and the only *theme* I wanted to think about was an ice-cold martini, straight up, two olives, no vermouth. My eyes wandered over toward the bar.

"Mary! Pay attention." Thom pounded the table with a fat fist. "You're the pastry chef at the hottest restaurant on the West Coast, not a bricklayer. I'm merely the controller. Can't you envision *something*?" The tone of his voice clearly implied that I had the imagination of a turnip. Having established the battle lines, he slouched lazily in his chair, the cut of his Armani jacket masterfully hiding his pudgy frame.

Envision something. Currently I was envisioning the cases of Valrhona chocolate I'd ordered in anticipation of making two hundred individual chocolate cakes. My food cost for the month of October would be a financial meltdown if I didn't convince him to stick with the original menu.

I was at a tactical disadvantage. My Ross wardrobe always paled in comparison with Thom's designer togs, but today I was more disheveled than usual. Anticipating a battle, I'd tried to boost my professional appearance by brushing my teeth and turning my apron to the clean side; but I'd been stirring caramel over a hot stovetop for the past two hours and was bedraggled and sweaty. I tried to contain the stench emanating from my armpits by holding my arms down at my sides, but I still must have smelled rank because Thom kept inching his chair away from me in discreet little hops. I was not in the mood to indulge Mrs. Gerson's ridiculous requests.

We sat at a table in the restaurant trying to finalize the menu. It was four o'clock, the lull between lunch and dinner service. In the background the kitchen hummed with activity as the crew sliced, diced, and whacked away in preparation for dinner. The dining room still bore the remnants of lunch service; a linen napkin here, a dirty wineglass there. Within an hour all the tables would be smartly dressed for dinner with white linens, precisely placed silverware, and gleaming wineglasses.

American Fare is a case study in what makes a successful restaurant. Firmly entrenched as the society hangout, we're chic but not snobbish, intellectual but not stuffy, fun but not giddy. On Tuesday nights when the opera is in season, you might see a man resplendent in a tuxedo seated at one table and a young dot-commer wearing a tee shirt at the table next to him. Neither looked out of place.

Thom tried again. "What about something along the lines of that exquisite spun sugar replica of City Hall you made for the reopening? The one that made the national news. Except this version would be a replica of the library."

"It took four months to make," I said flatly. "Mrs. Gerson's party is next week. I suggest something simple. The fall bounty is at its peak right now."

"Well, we can't just hand out apples, now can we?" Thom sneered.

I resisted the urge to stand up and pour my coffee over Thom's mousse-entombed hair.

Thom came on board when American Fare opened two years ago. It was mutual loathing at first sight. Shortly after his hire, he held a staff meeting to announce that he'd changed the spelling of his name. Although it was still pronounced "Tom," it was spelled with an "h" wedged in between the "T" and the "o." I always pronounce the "th" in his name—like Thumper—when he's not in the room, and a couple of times I've slipped up and actually "th'd" to his face. No wonder he thinks I'm a bitch.

He loves pampering and gossiping with the San Francisco socialites, and has so ingratiated himself that many of them now insist he help with the menu planning for their events. Mrs. Gerson is his personal favorite, a woman so obsessed with social climbing that I bet she has cleats on the soles of her Ferragamos.

"Persimmons are coming into season. What about my individual persimmon puddings with a Marsala zabaglione?" I suggested. "It'll be the talk of the town." When I was tired or bored, I tended to speak in clichés. Both applied in this case. I nonchalantly rolled down the sleeve of my uniform to hide a large blob of chocolate on my forearm.

Thom tried to narrow his eyes in frustration and anger but to no avail. A recent round of botox injections from a needle-happy plastic surgeon had left the upper half of his face with all the animation of a ventriloquist's dummy. "Mrs. Gerson is creating an *event*, Mary. I'm sure you can come up with something more exciting than persimmon pudding."

My persimmon pudding happens to be something to die for and Thom knew it. The next time he came sniffing around the kitchen begging for one of my boring persimmon puddings he could shove it up his snotty ass.

Shaking his head back and forth, he tsked-tsked as if deeply frustrated. All his worse fears had been realized. I did have the imagination of a turnip. Clearly I wasn't getting the point and he was going to have to spell it out for me.

"Must I repeat myself? *Theme*, Mary. Mrs. Gerson confided to me personally that she must make a splash with this party. All of the place cards have the guests' names printed like library cards, and for party favors she's handing out signed first editions of some children's book. Can't remember the name. Something about a boy who does magic tricks. Harvey Potts or something like that. I've never heard of this book, but Mrs. Gerson assures me this is the thing right now. Doesn't it sound like fun?"

I glared at him. "The last the time you used the word fun and Mrs. Gerson in the same sentence we catered her dog's birthday party."

"I remember that party." He sighed with satisfaction. "We got two," he waggled two chubby be-ringed fingers in my face, "two columns in the society pages."

"Those personalized dog biscuits made the restaurant smell like a Purina factory for a week," I snapped back. "As long as people pay for it, you'll agree to anything. And it's Harry Potter, you idiot."

"Why at some point in all our interactions do you stoop to name calling? We've gone down this road too many times for it to be even remotely amusing." He moued a yawn. "I handle the financial end, help with a little menu planning here and there." The smug tone of voice belied the insignificance of his role. "Your job is to make the desserts. Can we get cracking and decide on this menu? I haven't got all day. I was supposed to phone her over an hour ago with the menu change." He held up his watch and tapped it three times with one of his pudgy fingers.

With each tap, my back spasmed into an ever-increasing knot. No, beating him with the salt and pepper shakers wouldn't kill him fast enough. I should grab a chair and tap,

tap, tap his skull with it. But I swallowed my rage. I was hungry, I smelled bad, and I wanted to go home. Time to cut a deal.

"What about warm chocolate cakes with a blood orange mousse?" I suggested, thinking this might at least salvage some of my food cost. "Princess Michael of Kent ordered them last week and *loved* them. Remember, Thom?" I reminded him, adding a few strategic inflections of my own.

Thom got a thoughtful look in his eye, as if the aura of royalty was almost too much to resist. Then he must have realized how painfully easy those chocolate cakes were to make. Melt some chocolate, beat up a few egg whites, and voilà. Certainly not the hours of overtime on my part that he envisioned, which, since I was on salary, wouldn't cost the restaurant one cent extra.

"Come, Mary. Let's do something original that will leave San Francisco society talking for weeks. Something that will be written up in the society column the next day. Where's your sense of whimsy?"

Suffice it to say, my whimsy ran out the door screaming about three hours ago.

"Pear cardamom sorbet with chocolate-hazelnut tuilles," I suggested.

"Theme, Mary," he reminded me. "How about individual mille feuilles, sifted over with confectioner's sugar, with book titles on the top written in dark chocolate?"

"No way, Thom. Buches de noel, but instead of meringue mushrooms, make little squares of meringues to resemble books. Trees of Knowledge. Get it?"

Thom rolled his eyes. "Of course I got it. Too Christmasy, even without the mushrooms."

We fired dessert suggestions back and forth at each other for another ten minutes before finally compromising on individual chocolate boxes made up to look like books— dark chocolate for the top, bottom, and spine, white chocolate for the sides to resemble pages—filled with blood-orange mousse. Cutesy. Two hundred of these suckers. I loathe making cutesy desserts. Plus, tempering all that chocolate, working it back and forth with a spatula, determining when the chocolate was just at the right temperature to cut it without fracturing it. The knot in my back began throbbing violently in anticipation.

"Okay, okay. I'll do the goddamn boxes with the blood-orange mousse," I agreed wearily. "Call your Mrs. Gerson with the good news."

Thom didn't bother to hide a broad grin as he pushed himself away from the table. Why did I have the sick feeling that this was exactly what he wanted all along? In the background the janitor began moving the chairs in order to vacuum the dining room. I looked at my watch. One hour until service. I felt in my pockets for my car keys. I was so tired I was half tempted to go to my car without returning to the locker room for my backpack and wallet.

"Oh, Mary." Thom stopped his victory march across the dining room and called over one shoulder. "One small thing."

I waited.

"The names of literary classics piped on the front of each one. Make them all different. For fun."

"Fun," I repeated in a deadpan voice. There was that word again.

"You know, *Gone with the Wind* or *The Importance of Being Earnest*. Mrs. Gerson is a big Oscar Wilde fan."

I stared at him in horror. "And how am I supposed to fit," I counted quickly, "thirty-one letters, if you include spaces, on a five-inch by seven-inch piece of chocolate?"

"I have total faith in you," he said gaily and continued walking.

I shut my eyes in contemplation of the hours I'd spend hunched over a table, a paper cone filled with white chocolate, piping out literary titles on a rectangle the size of a postcard; truly, a labor of Hercules.

Yes, it was worth ten years in Q.

I opened my eyes and grabbed the salt and pepper shakers, but he was already halfway across the dining room, whistling "Cry Me a River."

Bastard.

Chapter 2

The morning of Mrs. Gerson's party my alarm clock went off at five. The weather had turned cold the weekend before and the tip of my nose and forehead were freezing, the only body parts not covered with down. As I turned on my bedside lamp to make sure I didn't fall back asleep, every muscle in my lower back screamed in violent protest. The hot light branded my eyelids until I couldn't stand it anymore, and I hauled my ass out of bed. On my way to the shower my calf muscles joined in the agony chorus and cramped in sympathy with my back. Yesterday had been an eighteen-hour day and even a scalding shower didn't rejuvenate me.

Shit, I thought, as my shoulder went into spasm while I pulled on a tee shirt. I'm getting too old for this. I felt ninety and near death.

The week before had been the proverbial nightmare. I'd worked an extra two hours every day, melting, tempering, and cutting out chocolate rectangles. Two days ago, just as I was ready to assemble the rectangles into their cutesy little mock-book form, I discovered someone had placed a hot stockpot next to the rack where I had stored the chocolate rectangles. All the sheetpans on the bottom of the rack had melted and rehardened, leaving the chocolate with a sickly bloom resembling bathtub scum. All that chocolate would have to be remelted, tempered again, and recut. It took every ounce of strength I had not to break down sobbing.

After making it crystal clear that if anyone got so much as within five feet of me and the rack with the chocolate on it I'd cut their hearts out with a clam knife, I fortified myself with a triple espresso every two hours and worked as if possessed by the devil himself. I'd managed to recoup most of the damage and had only two tasks left to do: make the mousse and pipe out the novel titles. I'd go in early before the kitchen crew arrived, finish up, and then go to my gym and soak for three hours. I've yet to use the exercise equipment. I belong to a gym for the Jacuzzi.

By five-thirty that morning, I was on the Bay Bridge, driving with one hand, eating cold toast with the other, hot coffee between my legs. I spent the entire drive racking my brains for the shortest novel titles I could think of. Anything longer than ten words didn't qualify. Jane Austen was good for three: *Emma*, *Sanditon*, and *Persuasion*. *Tom Jones* worked, *Vanity Fair* was good. *Bleak House*. *Jane Eyre*. The Victorians were winning hands down.

The restaurant had been closed the day before so that Davyd, party czar to S.F.'s elite, could work his magic on the dining room. He'd transformed our bistro French décor into an Art Deco extravaganza. Masses of blood-red tulips (where did he find tulips in October?) arced out of three-foot-high black lacquer vases scattered throughout the room. He'd replaced our tables with round tables for ten and covered them with black and white Harlequin-patterned tablecloths. For centerpieces he had grouped black-leather bound books, red fountain pens, quills, and wired-rimmed spectacles in a casual array that looks simple to achieve, but in reality is almost impossible to do right. Floor to ceiling-length scrolls of parchment lined the walls, each one penned in meticulous calligraphy with the first paragraph of a famous book. "It is a truth universally acknowledged…" from *Pride and Prejudice*. "In the late summer of that year we lived in a house…" from *A Farewell to Arms*. "In my younger and more vulnerable years my father gave me some advice…" from *The Great*

Gatsby. It was beautiful, but all that manufactured elegance made me uncomfortable. Time to enter the world I knew.

No matter how tired I am, I love entering the kitchen first thing in the morning before anybody else comes in. All the mean and nasty thoughts I'd had about lashing Thom's and Mrs. Gerson's bodies to Coit Tower and letting seagulls feast on their remains vanished.

Everything's dead quiet, the gleaming stainless steel tables polished and pristine, stovetop black, pots and pans hanging in their proper places, tile swept and mopped. In spite of the air of desertion and regimental order, there's a sense of expectancy. The soft chortle of boiling water hovers, the hint of vegetables hitting a hot sauté pan teases, the whack of knives on the chopping block waits. It's a wonderful tension of suspended sounds, sounds that in three hours would approach cacophony, but in the early morning light are waiting for the orchestra to begin. I feel as if I'm the only one in the theater and the orchestra is waiting to play the culinary version of the *1812 Overture.*

I threw my knife roll on a stainless steel table, made coffee, and went to the laundry closet in the back to get a chef's jacket and apron. Thursday is laundry delivery day and bags bursting with dirty laundry were piled all over the floor waiting to be picked up later that morning. God, the stench was terrible.

What in the hell had the janitors been cleaning up?

It smelled, well, fecal.

Breathing through my mouth to avoid the smell, I stepped on the laundry bags to reach the chef's jackets hanging up along the wall. No jacket in my size. Pulling on a size forty-four that hung on me like a shroud, I rolled up the sleeves and looked around for an apron; the only clean ones left were stacked on a high shelf above the jackets. I'm five foot nine, and I still couldn't reach them. Grabbing the wooden bar that held the jackets, I planted my foot on a laundry bag propped up against the wall and began to hoist myself up.

I stopped in my tracks.

Dirty laundry is spongy and gives when you step on it. This bag felt hard. Somebody probably put a few hams in there and planned on discreetly hauling them out the door with the rest of the laundry pick-up. How sneaky.

I knelt down to see what was inside. I held my breath; the stench emanating from the bag was rank enough to wilt lettuce.

The bag was closed tightly and elaborately knotted. Running back into the kitchen, I extracted a big chef's knife from my knife roll. Before entering the laundry closet I took a big gulp of fresh air and using the knife, sliced neatly through the knot. Placing my knife on the floor, I pulled open the bag with both hands. On top were a couple of kitchen towels that I quickly threw aside.

A human head filled the top of the bag.

I fought to keep my breakfast down while my mind spun round and round, trying to invent a rational explanation for why someone would be crunched up in a laundry bag.

I got down on my knees and slowly eased down the sides of the bag.

A small male Latino sat neatly folded into a cube inside the laundry bag, legs pinning his arms to his body in a compact vee, chin resting on his knees. An apron encircled his neck like a muffler. The apron strings had been wrapped around and around and then pulled tight, strangling him. I touched a shoulder. Hard as metal, cold as ice. His face, puffy and black with bruises, was unrecognizable. Except for one thing.

I'd know that haircut anywhere. Last week he'd come into work grinning from ear to ear with his black hair buzzed and streaked with blond stripes so that his head resembled a tiger. But he was proudest of a different part.

I knew what I would find, but I had to look. Razor-etched in the buzz cut across the back of his head was his name.

Perez.

I threw up my breakfast.

Once my stomach stopped heaving, I locked myself in the bathroom. First, I wanted to make sure that whoever killed Carlos Perez had left, and second I was debating whether or not to call my ex-husband, Jim.

Jim's a cop, a homicide inspector with S.F.P.D.

I wasn't sure whether the nasty cramps in my stomach were related to the retching or the thought that my ex-husband might be investigating this murder. Jim would be on my turf, my one haven where I could banish any thoughts of him with mind-numbing labor. My reaction to the divorce had been bitter and angry, something I'd refused to analyze in any depth despite months of therapy.

Common sense told me that it would be a plus to have Jim assigned to the case. It might save me from hassles later on. As I listened for any sounds that might be the noises of the killer roaming around the kitchen, I did some mental volleyball: "Do I call him?" "Should I call 911?"

After some minutes of silence, punctuated by ugly flashes of Carlos folded up like a bloody chicken, I made a decision. I'd call 911. I'd probably have to sign a statement and that would be the end of it. There were lots of homicide cops in S.F.P.D.; the likelihood of Jim being assigned to the case was nil.

I washed my face a dozen times and used my finger to brush my teeth with bacterial soap. I eased the bathroom lock open and stuck my head through the door opening.

Silence.

I slunk along the corridors of the restaurant, my ears on high alert for any sounds other than my own shallow panting.

When I was sure I was alone, I sprinted across the dining room and called 911 from the reservation line. The phone kept slipping from my sweaty palm. It took me five attempts before I was able to punch in 911 and another five attempts to speak coherently. After the dispatcher ascertained I wasn't hurt and that the murderer wasn't on the premises, she told me to open the doors and wait for the beat cops.

I followed her instructions to the letter; I opened wide the front doors to the restaurant for a possible escape route, then ran to a banquette the farthest distance possible from Carlos' battered body, and waited for the beat cops to arrive. I brought my knees up to my forehead and cried, shivering like a bowl of Jell-O during an earthquake.

When O'Connor entered the restaurant my stomach did a threatening flip-flop.

I was sitting in the banquette, packing and unpacking my knife roll, realigning the knives, small to big, taking them out again, sharpening them on the steel, putting them back into their slots big to small, over and over again.

O'Connor was Jim's partner.

My face was still wet from tears, and I had streaks on my arms from where I'd wiped my nose. Seeing O'Connor staring at me across the room with a glare he usually reserves for murderers, I stopped dead just as I was about to scrape my cleaver against the steel. If Jim walked through that door, I'd slice my wrists.

To my great surprise and relief, however, another detective named Chang followed in O'Connor's wake. The two of them stood there for about five minutes, conferring with the beat cops. I saw O'Connor gesture with his head toward me and then hike a thumb in the direction of the laundry closet. Chang went into the kitchen and O'Connor came over to where I was sitting.

With a brief glance, he slid into the booth. S.F.P.D. must have gotten some decent funding because O'Connor began setting up a laptop.

Without looking up he began firing questions at me.

"So, the dispatcher says you knew the victim. Who was it?"

His large hands poised over the tiny keyboard keys looked cartoonish. O'Connor's laptop made sharp clicking sounds in beat with the crisp tone in his voice.

I slid the cleaver into its sleeve and rolled up the knife roll. "Hello, O'Connor. Nice to see you, too," I said, dragging out the last "o."

O'Connor stopped typing and flicked a glance at me as if to say, you know the game, you can do better than that.

"Yeah, he worked at the restaurant," I mumbled to the tabletop. The reality of my co-worker's murder nearly robbed me of speech. I grabbed my knife roll off the table and clutched it to my chest, seeking comfort, like a child clutching its favorite blanket. I closed my eyes.

O'Connor's fingers grazed the fabric of my chef's jacket and I felt a gentle shake of my shoulder.

"Come on, Ryan, what do you mean? A lot of people work here. Did he work directly under you? What's the story?"

"His name is…" Carlos' face, beaten beyond recognition, his name etched into the back of his head, flashed in my mind and the tears started rolling again. "O'Connor, I've just discovered an employee of mine beaten to a pulp and strangled with an apron. Cut me some slack. Please."

I turned sideways in the booth and curled up in a fetal position with my arms over my head to escape his questions, hoping this was a grisly nightmare, the outcome of too many fourteen-hour days.

I didn't notice he'd left until I heard the loud wheeze of the banquette as he sat down. I looked at him through the aperture of my armpit. O'Connor pointed to a water glass filled with brandy.

"Drink it," he ordered.

"You're n…not supposed to g…g…give alcohol to people in shock," I sobbed.

"You're not in shock, you're on a crying jag. I'm going to check out that laundry closet. When I come back, I want to find that glass empty. Then we talk." He marched in the direction of the laundry closet, leaving a wake of heel marks on our highly polished wood floor.

What O'Connor lacked in height he made up for in breadth. His broad shoulders, beefy arms, and stocky legs screamed Irish farmer. There are generally two types of Irish, the red-haired, blue-eyed variety, and the Black Irish, the reputed descendants of Spanish soldiers marooned on the Irish coast after the British defeat of the Spanish Armada in 1588. O'Connor is Black Irish. Although the Irish generally don't spoil a good story by telling the truth, he certainly was swarthy enough to be the descendant of some Spanish sailor— dark eyes, black unruly hair, and an olive cast to his skin.

The liquor was a stupid idea and I knew I'd pay for it later. I'd had five hours' sleep the night before, discovered a dead body, and just thrown up my breakfast. But O'Connor had been right. The sugar content of the brandy broke the crying fit.

By the time O'Connor came back I'd finished my drink and felt relatively calm. He carried a tray with a coffee pot on it and a couple of cups. Putting the tray down on the table, he filled the cups and handed me one.

"Here. Drink some coffee or you're going to get plastered from all that booze."

I hated myself but I had to ask. "Where's Jim? Why isn't he here?"

O'Connor slid back into the booth and began fiddling with the salt and pepper shakers on the table. When he finally answered his voice was curt. "He transferred to Internal Affairs. His new wife didn't like him working homicide."

His big hand caressed his jaw like he had a toothache. Looking at me, his hand stopped suddenly and fell limp on the table. "Christ, Mary, you look like hell."

O'Connor and I hadn't seen each other in almost a year. Catching my reflection in the mirror above the bar, I saw a woman with angry green eyes glaring back at me. Attractively slender had morphed into haggard and gaunt. In an act of pure self-destruction, I'd gone to one of those haircuts-for-ten-bucks places and ordered them to chop off all of my hair.

It looked like someone cut it with poultry shears. I couldn't remember the last time I'd worn makeup.

"I discovered a body. Lighten up," I said.

"This has nothing to do with that body back there, Ryan. You've lost at least twenty pounds. What in God's name did you do to your hair?" he demanded.

I looked in the mirror again and turned away. "It's been rough," I mumbled.

We sat there for a few seconds in silence. O'Connor poised his hands over his laptop. "We'll talk about you and Jim later. Let's start over. Are you ready to tell me what happened?"

Grabbing the coffee cup with both hands, I took a few tiny sips and began with brandy-inspired bravado. "You know this time of year is sheer hell. The restaurant has been closed for a couple of days for this bitch of a charity function tonight. I came in early to finish up the desserts."

Beginning with the simultaneous openings of both the symphony and the opera in the second week of September—known in the vernacular as "hell week"—the San Francisco social whirl continues at a frantic pace until after the New Year. Pre-symphony gigs, post-opera wing-dings, charity whatsits, most of which demanded show-stopping desserts. For me this meant working a slew of twelve- to fourteen-hour days. I went to work in the dark, came home in the dark, went back to work in the dark, an endless cycle. I literally never saw the sun. That was how it was going to be until after January 1st.

"What time did you arrive?"

"About six."

"Anyone else here?" he asked.

"No, I was alone. I went into the laundry closet to get a chef's jacket and an apron. I stepped on a bag of towels on the floor…" I stopped, realizing I'd been standing on a corpse. I bit my lip in an effort not to break down. "It…it didn't feel like towels," I said lamely. "I thought somebody had stolen something and concealed it in the bag. I couldn't undo the knot, so I got a knife and cut the string. There were a couple of kitchen towels on top—"

My bravado deserted me and I started crying again. My hands began shaking so badly that hot coffee spilled over the sides and burned my fingers.

O'Connor took the coffee cup away from me and let me weep for a few minutes. Then he pulled a large white handkerchief out of his shirt pocket and handed it to me.

"Here, wipe your eyes and blow your nose," he ordered. "Then describe the laundry bag, where it was, and the position of the body."

I cleaned myself up, took several deep breaths, and recited mechanically, "The bag was against the far wall. I pulled down the sides of the bag and…found him. His face was bruised and distorted. Bad bruises, like someone had beaten him with a frying pan. The laces of the apron had been wrapped around his neck a few times and then pulled real tight. When I realized what had happened, I…I…threw up my breakfast all over the laundry closet, then somehow got it together to call 911."

"Okay, so that's your knife on the floor and you used it to open the laundry bag, right?"

I nodded.

"Anything else?" he demanded.

"That's it," I whispered. I picked up the coffee cup again, clutching it with both hands.

"The dispatcher said you knew the victim. Did you look in his pockets for some I.D.?" The soft clicking of the computer keys was getting on my nerves.

"I didn't need to look for I.D. I knew who it was."

O'Connor stopped typing. He looked at me askance. "I saw the body, Ryan. His own mother wouldn't recognize him."

I remembered the name cut into the hair. "It was Carlos Perez, one of my pastry assistants. His name's etched with a razor into the back of his head."

Carlos was a chubby young man who, along with his brother Gilberto, had fled El Salvador to escape the war. Carlos always sang and joked his way through his shift, despite working two jobs to support his family. Carlos and Gilberto had worked with me previously at a couple of restaurants as dishwashers. When American Fare opened, he had been promoted to the pastry staff based largely on his willingness to do any job with a big grin on his face. Peel two cases of apples. Sure, no problema, *Señora*. Pit cherries for three hours. I'll do it right now.

I had liked Carlos very much.

O'Connor scrolled up and down a few times. "Give me a rough time line."

Should I tell him about locking myself in the bathroom? It was perfectly legitimate to hide from the killer. I'd leave the part out about debating Jim's involvement. The issue was moot.

"I got here about six, made coffee, discovered the body, and then locked myself in the bathroom for awhile," I said.

The typing stopped. "Locked yourself in the bathroom?" The tiniest smile hinted on his lips. "For how long and why?"

"Get that look off your face, O'Connor," I huffed. "How was I to know if the killer was or wasn't in the restaurant? If you'd just found a co-worker beaten to death, you'd have hightailed it to the bathroom, too."

O'Connor wiped the smirk off his face. "So how long?"

I thought back to how long I'd perched on the toilet making sure my feet didn't show. As if that would stop someone from beating me to death with a sauté pan. "I'd guess about fifteen minutes. It's hard to estimate time when you're nearly pissing in your underwear with terror."

The smile came back.

"Fair enough, Ryan." He scanned back a couple of pages and frowned. "Why were these bags all over the floor?"

"We go through tons of laundry. There's no place else to put it. It piles up until the laundry is picked up. Today's delivery day."

"So why did you step on the bag?"

My palms started to sweat again. It was hard to hold my coffee cup. The booze was seeping into my system, but instead of becoming drunk, I felt like I was coming down with an instant case of the flu. "I couldn't reach the aprons, they were too high up."

"Think. Anything about the room strike you?"

"The smell," I said flatly. "It smelled like shit."

"Yeah, that happens sometimes. The body lets loose when you die. What door did you come in, front or back? Was the lock forced?"

"I came in the front door. The lock was okay."

"Sounds like an inside job. What about the kitchen, the restaurant? Anything look like it had been stolen or disturbed?"

I let my mind run over the layout of the restaurant. If you come in from the front door the bar is along the left wall, and a black baby grand piano squats in the far left corner of the room. The kitchen is to the right, with all the sauté stations fully exposed. The pastry section extends back into the kitchen in the ell created by the stairs that go up to the office. Behind the pastry section and down the hall are the walk-in refrigerator and the freezers. Opposite the freezers is the laundry closet.

I pictured my movements before I found the body. "No, the kitchen and the dining room looked fine, nothing out of the ordinary. I didn't go upstairs."

"What's upstairs?"

"The office, the safe, computer equipment."

"Who locks up?" he demanded.

I started to take another sip of coffee, and then stopped myself. I needed to eat something before I had any more coffee.

"Well, normally Juan, the maître d', locks up. I think I left about ten last night, maybe nine-thirty?" I guessed and, against my better judgment, finished off my coffee.

"You don't know when you got off work?" He sounded annoyed.

"It was an eighteen-hour day," I snapped back.

"What about everyone else?"

"I don't know. When I left, Brent, the chef, was still here. Ron Chung, the sous chef, plus the kitchen staff. We were prepping for this party tonight. Davyd, the party organizer, and a few of his staff were putting the finishing touches on the dining room. Oh, Thom, too."

"Thom?" O'Connor, his wife Moira, Jim, and I had been customers at the restaurant often and he and Brent were on a first-name basis, but O'Connor had never had the good fortune to run into Thom.

"The controller. Fussy, pushy guy with a Napoleon complex. He and I don't get along." The clicking of the computer keys was starting to put me to sleep. I yawned.

The clicking stopped.

"Stay awake, Ryan," he warned. "Any way we can track which employees were here?"

"Everybody except for Juan, Brent, Thom, and Davyd's crew should have punched a time card. The time clock is just outside the laundry closet, but that's worthless if you're looking for a head count. People wait for their friends to get off. I saw at least three guys who weren't scheduled to work hanging outside the back door last night."

O'Connor grimaced. This type of homicide makes forensics almost worthless. A public place where a ton of suspects have a perfect right to be.

"And what about this Davyd guy? What's his last name?"

"Doesn't have a last name. Like Cher." The coffee wasn't working. I crossed my arms out in front of me and put my head down.

"Stay awake, Ryan," he ordered and was about to ask another question when a panicky voice screeched across the empty restaurant.

"What's going on here? Who's in charge? I demand to see the officer in charge!"

Chapter 3

Chef Brent Brown had arrived.

I stood up and waved my arm to catch Brent's attention. He saw me and plowed his way through the two officers guarding the door.

Brent's always on someone's top-ten chef list in the United States. He had realized early on that a restaurant must be "sold" if it's going to survive year after year. In the old days you relied on food to sell a place. Now a restaurant must have good food, a superb florist, and great press. Brent courts the media shamelessly, and, as a result, he's not only a San Francisco personality, but nationally known as well. I thought the four-page spread on his home in *House Beautiful* was over the top, but right after that he had the money to open American Fare. Shows what I know about marketing and finance.

As usual, Brent wore the latest Italian couture. It didn't suit him. Italian looks best on dark, slim, young men with no waists and nice butts. Brent is blond and heavyset, and has an ass that would best be described as bovine. He's put on weight in the last couple of years and his features border on the porcine.

He ran up to our booth, his arms chopping the air with every syllable he uttered. The Italian leather jacket creaked in protest against each big arm movement.

"What's going on here? The benefit, the benefit! I have to start dinner right now," he screamed.

"It's okay, guys," O'Connor reassured the cops chasing after Brent. Both of them were gripping their nightsticks with such fervor that O'Connor warned them again. "Fellas, it's *cool*. I know this guy." They glared at an oblivious Brent and reluctantly walked back to the front door.

"Chef Brown," O'Connor said in a grave voice. "Someone's been murdered in the restaurant. I'll have to ask you some questions."

Brent's lips opened in the surprised pout of dead fish. He seemed incapable of moving or saying anything.

O'Connor slid out from the table and motioned Brent to sit down.

"Mary, move over. Give Chef Brown some room. I'll go get more coffee. Morales," O'Connor yelled to one of the officers guarding the door and beckoned him with his hand. "Please stay here and see if Ms. Ryan or Mr. Brown need anything while I'm gone. Back in a minute." He walked off with the empty coffee pot.

While Morales stood guard, Brent woodenly removed his jacket, hung it carefully on the back of a dining chair, and sidled his way into the booth. He must have come from the hairdresser; his hair was highlighted to mask the gray and styled to hide the bald spot at the back of his head. I guess he wanted to look his best for the socialites this evening. He turned to me, his face pinched now with worry.

"Mary, do you know who it was? Was it a robbery?" His voice barely reached me even though we were only eight inches apart.

I put my hand on his shoulder. Even through his shirt I could feel his muscles twitching.

"It was Carlos Perez, Brent. And I'm afraid—" I stopped.

At the sound of Carlos' name, Brent's face blanched as white as the tablecloth. Giant perspiration stains immediately soaked the armpits of his shirt.

Oh, my God, I thought. He's having a heart attack.

"Are you okay?" I yelled and seized his wrist to see if he had any pulse.

Brent shuddered and pulled his wrist away from me with a snap. He grabbed the edge of the tablecloth to wipe his face. The meticulously constructed sculpture of books, pens, and quills crashed into a distinctly lumpy pile.

"I'm fine." He straightened his shoulders and ran a hand through his hair. "What's the matter with you?" Refusing to look me in the eye, he grabbed my coffee and began slurping it.

Brent and I have worked together a long time. He isn't a friend—his tendency to sleep with every woman under the age of twenty-five precludes friendship as far as I am concerned—but there's a deep bond and mutual respect between us forged over a lot of fourteen-hour days.

We met seven years ago. Fresh from Denver, he was hired to take a mediocre prime rib restaurant whose heyday was circa 1958 and "modernize" it. He fired the whole staff except for me. I didn't have high hopes—the man walked in wearing a cowboy hat. I gave him two months before he was canned. Within two years he'd received the James Beard Award, the Oscar equivalent in the cooking world, for Most Outstanding New Chef.

Having proved himself in the kitchen, Brent has been swept up in the latest craze to consume the cooking world: the celebrity chef. He hired the same agent who represents Barbara Walters and before you could say *pommes frites*, numerous articles featuring him appeared in the cooking mags. Then he went mainstream with the spread in *House Beautiful*, and last time I spoke with him, he was negotiating for his own television show. The upside of all this is that it gives the restaurant continued national recognition and keeps our tables filled every night. The downside is that he bends over backward to accommodate star-fuckers like Mrs. Gerson, who cares little about the food and more about her press clippings.

I find this frantic grab for fame bizarre. Every now and then he drags me into these promotional forays. If I don't medicate myself beforehand with massive amounts of Benadryl, I break out in hives from nerves. I've gotten a reputation for being ultra cool in these situations when in reality I'm drugged to the eyeballs.

I've tried to ignore this rapacious self-aggrandizement because I'm eternally grateful to Brent. He's one of the few chefs I've met who doesn't think pastry is the shit can of the kitchen. The prevailing opinion among chefs is that those that can do, and those that can't do pastry. I chose pastry after butchering seven sides of beef in one day. The smell of blood was etched into my nasal cavities for days. Three hundred pounds of chocolate lying on a table doesn't make you want to throw up. It also doesn't have eyes.

Before he and I hooked up, I'd done time in too many kitchens to count where I'd had to adopt this bitchy, balls-the-size-of-grapefruits attitude to get any respect. I was called *Señora Cojones* behind my back. I didn't care. It saved my eggs from getting smashed when someone threw a side of beef into the walk-in or having my butter smell like fish because a pantry cook placed cooling fish stock next it. Too bad it hadn't saved my chocolate boxes. I must be losing my touch.

In the last year, however, Brent's sorely tested my allegiance. The restaurant has struggled to maintain the quality and innovation we're famous for because he just doesn't have the time to both manage a kitchen and pose for publicity shots. And after the week I'd had indulging Mrs. Gerson's quest for fame, I was not feeling too kindly toward him.

I grabbed my coffee cup back.

"Brent, I'm not some twenty-year-old you can bullshit. What in the hell is going—" Before I could finish my sentence, O'Connor reappeared with the coffee. By this time Brent had regained his composure and now only looked pale, a reasonable response under the circumstances.

O'Connor poured Brent a cup. "Chef Brown, I'd appreciate it if you'd have a cup of coffee, calm down, and wait for me here. I've a few more questions to ask Ms. Ryan, then I'll be back and explain what's happened."

Brent looked up at O'Connor and nodded, his solid midwestern frame slack with fatigue. The only thing holding him upright was the back of the red leather booth.

"Ryan," O'Connor barked and jerked his head in the direction of the kitchen. Before I got up I turned my head so that O'Connor couldn't see my face and tried to make eye contact with Brent. He ignored me and began restacking the pieces of the centerpiece.

I grabbed my knife roll and followed O'Connor into the one area of the kitchen that wasn't teeming with police technicians. What a mess. Camera and video equipment, saucers overflowing with smoldering cigarettes despite department orders not to smoke at crime scenes, and half-filled coffee cups littered the stainless steel tables. The janitors would have to scrub for hours to clean this up.

I leaned against a five-foot-high stack of sheet pans and hugged my knife roll to my chest. I'd never felt so exhausted in all my life.

"O'Connor, can I go home now? I've told you everything I know about the murder. I'm so tired even the tiny hairs in my ears hurt. If I think of anything else, I'll call you. I promise."

O'Connor scowled and loosened his tie. "Most likely this is a simple case of some guy finding out that a co-worker was screwing his wife. Brown has a reputation with the ladies, doesn't he?"

I had often entertained O'Connor with gossip about the restaurant. Right now my amusing little tidbits about Brent's love life seemed unwise. From my vantage point in the kitchen, I could see Brent clutching his coffee cup like a lifesaver. Morales stood next to him, stiff with authority.

"Mmm," I mumbled.

"Did he ever hit on you?"

"No," I said wearily. "He'd never jeopardize our professional relationship by having an affair with me. Besides, he likes them young and blond, neither of which applies to me. Carlos' wife doesn't fit the bill either if that's where you're headed. She's seven months pregnant. Can I go now?"

"For the second time, no. You'll still need to come down to the station in the morning to make a statement, but I might want to ask you more questions while everything's fresh in your mind. Stay put." He turned his back on me and went back out to the dining room to talk with Brent.

The liquor and lack of food were working a number on my body. Sweat ran down my back in tiny rivulets. The snot streaks on my arm had dried to the consistency of cement. I needed a shower and a nap. Time to start cashing in some of those chips I hoped I'd earned as the wife of a cop, albeit ex-wife. Summoning every bit of energy I had left, I followed him out of the kitchen. I caught him halfway across the dining room and thumped him on the shoulder.

"I'm going now."

He spun around and pointed his finger in my face.

I hate that.

"Ryan, don't move your ass one inch. You're the premiere witness in this case. Don't make me get official with you."

"Get official. You know where I live." I walked out of the restaurant.

Chapter 4

The entrance to the alley had been cordoned off with yellow crime-scene tape. Ignoring the obnoxious questions of the crowd, I walked over to the far end of the alley where the cops had rounded up the kitchen crew.

The majority of the employees in any kitchen in America are Latino. I'm talking at least ninety percent. We always have a few recent graduates from my old alma mater, École d'Epicure, but they stay only long enough to pick the brains of senior staff and then they move on to the next high-profile chef. The staff turnover in any restaurant is phenomenal. Without Latinos the restaurant industry would collapse. They work their asses off, get their paychecks, and aren't interested in moving on. Most of the Latinos working in American Fare had been there from the day we opened.

Huddled up against a wall, their brown faces terrified, I knew this would be a tremendous ordeal for every one of them. They were largely from Guatemala or El Salvador, countries where the police hauled people away, no questions asked. Even though all of them were legal, the kind of brute force that officials wielded in their countries made them fear any kind of authority.

Juan, the maître d', was among the crowd. As soon as he saw me he beckoned me over. "What happened? A robbery? They won't tell us anything."

Everyone stopped talking.

"Didn't they tell you what happened?"

Fifteen people shook their heads.

I swallowed hard. "Someone's been murdered in the restaurant."

"Who is it, who is it?" several voices shouted at me. I searched for Carlos' brother, Gilberto, in the crowd. He worked under me, too, and was on the schedule for that day. I couldn't see him. I didn't feel I should say anything until his family was told.

I shrugged my shoulders to indicate I didn't know. "They'll have to question everyone. Juan, I told them to talk with you, that you usually lock up. You'll be here for hours. Ask the officers if you guys can at least have a cup of coffee." The panic in the Latinos' faces multiplied.

As exhausted as I was, I knew I had to say something.

"Hey, it's all right," I said to the crowd. "The police are just going to ask a few questions. No big deal." It didn't make a bit of difference; their backs were stiff with fear.

I turned back to Juan. "They're so scared, could you please talk to them and let them know that it's just routine. Assure them nothing's going to happen to them."

He sighed. "It won't make any difference. To them, any police officer is the enemy. When I saw the police tape I knew it was serious. I tried to phone Thom but he's not home. I will call Mrs. Gerson and explain that due to unfortunate circumstances beyond our control, we will have to cancel her party. No doubt she will be most distraught, but I will tell her that we will only be postponing the event and that perhaps in light of the situation, we might be able to renegotiate the price of the meal. I am sure we will come to some sort of satisfactory arrangement."

In spite of my fatigue, I smiled. How clever of him. The one thing I've learned about rich people is that they are, without exception, incredibly cheap.

"Thank you, Juan. I'm going home now. Please let Brent know that you called Mrs. Gerson with the bad news. He'll be ecstatic he didn't have to talk to her. If you remember, call me this evening with an update on when we can reopen."

"Of course, Mary. I shall call about seven. Also, I shall call the wait staff and tell them not to come in."

Juan's affected formal courtesy normally irritates the shit out of me. He has cultivated this stagey, Ricardo Montalban-like persona over the years to establish credibility. To my ears he usually sounds like he's hawking used Lincoln town cars. After today's events, however, it was a comforting refrain.

I hoisted my knife roll over my shoulder, lied to the officer at the crime scene tape saying that O'Connor had given me his blessing to leave, and muscled my way through the crowd. I had to get out of the restaurant before they took away the beaten body that had been Carlos Perez.

Driving home, I broke every speed limit between San Francisco and Albany. When Jim and I were married we lived in the Avenues. The minute I got divorced, I moved back across the bay as far away from the fog and my failed marriage as possible. From the divided proceeds of our house I'd bought a minuscule two-bedroom cottage in Albany, two minutes away from my mother. I didn't exactly move back home, but I came pretty close without exactly putting my sheets on her bed.

My inertia after the divorce was total. My kitchen still sported the faded pink-and-green rooster wallpaper, with pink appliances to match, no less, that the previous owner had put up in 1955. The tone of the house matched my state of mind these days—faded and old.

Before I even took off my coat, I curled up on the couch and dialed my mother's phone number. I dozed for a couple of seconds while waiting for her to pick up the phone.

"Mom, it's Mary."

"Mary, how are you?" Her voice was pleasantly surprised and upbeat. She'd be in the breakfast nook, a game of solitaire on the kitchen table.

"Uh, not so hot. There was a murder at the restaurant this morning. I wanted to tell you before you heard it on the news."

I pictured the shock on her face, saw her fumbling for her glasses, as if better vision would somehow clear up the confusion.

I considered my mother a viable candidate for sainthood. She raised my sister and me more or less on her own, when nurses made diddlysquat. I remember her routinely working nine, ten days in a row without a day off. Also in those days, divorced women were stigmatized, basically considered one small step above fallen women. She dated several men over the years, and while many of them might have made good husbands, none of them would have made good fathers. She met my stepfather when I was fifteen and finally found the happiness she so richly deserved, and my sister and I finally got the stability we so desperately needed.

I went through the gory details with her, trying to be as brief as I could without sounding curt. Being a nurse, details about corpses don't faze her much.

"Have you called Jim?" she asked hesitantly.

"No," I said peevishly. "It's none of his business."

"Mary, Jim's a homicide detective." As if I needed reminding. "It might be wise to let him know what's going on."

"He's not even in homicide anymore. Don't worry. O'Connor's on the case." I hoped she wouldn't press the issue any further. She and O'Connor knew each other and had a mutual admiration society going. No such luck, of course.

"Mary, I know how you feel about him. I felt that way when your father left me. But this is eating you up. Your…"

I interrupted her, "Mom, hurt doesn't describe what this divorce did to me. Two years ago I was considered a nice person. I was even happy. Now, I'm mean and bitter. My staff at work is on the verge of mutiny because I'm so sarcastic. A job I once loved, I now hate. I don't even garden anymore."

She paused, took a deep breath, and exhaled that poignant "mom" breath. I was in trouble.

"I think your anger is out of bounds." Her speech became slower and slower, and she picked her words with care. "Don't you think you should see someone again? Maybe this is bigger than you and Jim. Perhaps this anger you feel is related to your father and me divorcing..." My mother's voice trailed off and I could feel her guilt over the phone.

The parents and children of divorce—or broken homes, don't you love that word—do this guilt dance. The parents blame themselves for not trying harder, the kids think that if they were better kids the divorce wouldn't have happened. In our case, my mother and I knew that divorcing my father was the smartest thing she ever did. Yet the doubts are there, whispering in the back of our mind in times of crisis.

"If I were on trial for murder I wouldn't ask for Jim's help."

There wasn't much she could say to that. We sat in silence for a minute.

"I'm sorry, Mary."

"Mom, I know you're sorry. I'm sorry too. We're all sorry together. Except for Jim, of course, he has his nice little family now." I stopped, realizing too late I'd gone over the line. I pushed my palm hard against my forehead, trying to get back in control. "Let's drop it, okay?" I fought back tears.

"I'm worried about you. Let me come over. You sound like you are in bad shape."

I love my mother to death, but I just couldn't handle one more person, one more conversation, one more single thing.

"Please don't. I just need some sleep. I'll be over sometime tomorrow afternoon. I've got to give a statement to the police in the morning. Afterwards I'll come right over. I promise. We'll have a cup of tea."

I hung up, hating myself. The worst thing about this divorce was that it had unleashed a Mr. Hyde persona from within me I never knew existed. Once witty, I was now caustic. Wry had mutated into bitter. It seemed that I couldn't have a conversation without saying something snide. Now my mother would fret all day and into the night worrying about me. The worst thing was that I knew she was right. The horrible crunchy rumblings I got in my stomach thinking about Jim were the same horrible crunchy rumblings I used to feel as a ten-year-old knowing that my father wasn't coming home.

I couldn't deal with this now. Freud and murder all in one day was too much. In penance, I called a florist and paid a premium to have flowers delivered to her within an hour.

Sleep seemed more imperative than a shower. I closed the curtains and climbed into bed with my clothes on. I was just about to shut my eyes when I realized I hadn't called my sister, Nora. I redialed the florist and asked them to scribble a note on the enclosed card to my mother that in addition to being sorry, would she please call Nora and give her the details. Hoping I had finally fulfilled my familial obligations, I fell into a killer sleep.

I'd slept for a couple of hours when the phone rang. I moved to answer it. In addition to the aches and pains left over from yesterday, a monster hangover, two hundred tap-shoes strong, was tapping out "River Dance" in the back of my head. I slowly eased myself back into my pillows. Whoever it was could leave a message. I fell back into a light sleep during the usual clicks and beeps, and then a familiar voice boomed through the answering machine.

"Ryan, get your ass out of bed. Right now. I know you're there. I've got questions that need answering right away."

He started shouting "get up, get up" into the receiver. I knew this man, he'd keep it up till the tape ran out.

As he had intended, my stupor turned into pure adrenaline. I was going to get up all right and there wouldn't be any prisoners. I picked up the phone in a fury.

"O'Connor, this is harassing a witness. I was asleep, you bastard," I shouted into the phone.

He laughed. "That's what I like about you, Ryan, always ready for a fight."

"Let's be honest, O'Connor. You don't like me. You just need something from me."

"Right on both counts, I don't like you and I do need something from you. Answer my questions and I'll leave you alone. Hang up on me and I'll come across the bridge and ask you my questions in person. To say I'm pissed off at you is an understatement. Talk to me and you can go back to your beauty sleep."

I debated hanging up, but knowing him he'd drive across the bridge and track me down like a dog. I smelled, and my mouth felt like I'd been eating stale Cheetos in my sleep. I stared at myself in the dresser mirror. My hair was mashed to one side from my pillow and, despite the nap, bags as plump and dark as mission figs sat under my eyes. Worst of all, I looked old. Beauty sleep. Who was he kidding? I didn't want anyone seeing me in this state.

The thought of making O'Connor drive across the bridge during rush hour *was* mighty tempting, however.

"Okay, I'm sorry," I apologized. "I'm not playing any games. I had to leave before they took out the body. I just had to."

"If you weren't my best friend's wife, I'd haul you in right now," he threatened.

"Ex-wife, remember?"

"Yeah. The coroner is giving me a rough estimate of two in the morning for the time of death. Brown says he left the restaurant at midnight. I talked to his wife and she confirms it. Do you think she'd lie for him?"

I thought for a minute about Brent's wife.

Sharon Brown. A very unhappy woman. I've rarely heard her utter something that wasn't sarcastic, most of it directed at her husband. She obviously knew about his affairs. In addition to her waspish tongue, she'd gained a tremendous amount of weight with her kids and, lately, her clothes and hair were dirty half the time I saw her.

And yet, I've been to several garden parties at her immaculate, elegant house. She designs and plants everything herself, from the flower beds lush with foxgloves and delphiniums to an organic vegetable garden that boasts six different kinds of basil. I often wondered, what's going on here? To add to the mystery, she's a wonderful mother. Her kids are smart, unpretentious, and affectionate. Since Brent works about seventy hours a week, I give her all the credit.

"They've got a pretty rotten marriage," I admitted. "She knows he cheats on her. I've worked with him for the last seven years and he always has one or two on the side. She pretty much hates him, but the kids adore him and she'd do anything for her children. So if exposing her husband as a lying sack of shit would hurt her children, yes, she'd lie."

"At first glance it looks like a crime of passion. Perez's face was beaten to a pulp. The coroner thinks the bruising is consistent with some sort of flat object hitting his face. Your description of the frying pan probably isn't too far off. The forensic guys are testing every sauté pan in the restaurant. And the strangulation fits too—grab an apron and finish him off. But the business with the laundry bag has me stumped. Also, you'd think some argument that got out of hand would be settled by a jab in the belly. I haven't met a Latino yet who doesn't carry a knife. The laundry bag makes it look premeditated. It's neat. No blood, just haul him out the door. Any ideas on who'd want to kill Perez?"

The headache ruled out any serious mental overtime, but this one was a no-brainer.

"No, everyone liked him. Nice guy, hard worker." When Carlos discovered that Jim and I were getting a divorce, he'd given me a flower every day for two months to cheer me up. God knows whose garden he was pilfering blooms from, but his thoughtfulness saved me from many a bleak hour.

"Did he chase women?"

"The guys don't talk about that stuff with me. Ask his brother or some of the other Latinos. I doubt he was fooling around. He was always bringing me in pictures of his kids, saying how proud he was of them, how they were going to be real Americans when they grew up."

Remembering those photos brought a lump to my throat. His two boys were proudly displaying their Forty-Niner football jerseys. His one-year-old daughter wore a frilly pink dress with an enormous lace collar that just about swallowed her sweet little smile.

"Ever meet his wife?"

"No, I've just seen pictures of her. Pretty. Young."

"Morales says Brown practically peed in his pants when you told him about Perez. Is that true?"

A shiver went down my back. Instinctively, I tried to minimize Brent's reaction. "Yeah, he seemed upset. I mean, so was I."

"You have an excuse, you discovered the body. Morales thinks Brown's reaction was inappropriate. Knowing Brown's history, I need to nail down some facts. I'm going to assume his wife is lying. If Brown wasn't home around the time of Perez's death, where was he? Who's his current girlfriend? Out with her name."

I lay there mute, holding the phone with one hand while bunching the covers around my neck like a noose with the other. I knew I had to tell him, but something held me back. It's one thing if everyone in the restaurant knows you're sleeping with the chef; I imagine it has a certain cachet to these silly girls. They wouldn't feel so smug once the police reduced it to what it was, a middle-aged man getting his rocks off.

Brent's proclivity for screwing the help was the source of our only serious arguments. A few years ago he and I practically came to blows over a pastry assistant who quit when she realized she was just one in a long line of many. Since then, we had a tacit agreement: the pastry staff was off limits.

"Name or names?" I knew I sounded coy but couldn't seem to stop myself.

"Ms. Ryan, this is a homicide investigation. One of your employees was murdered last night. Is this getting through to you? I'm not arresting Brown, I just want to know where he was. No funny games or witticisms. I want names. NOW!" He punched that last word through the phone so forcefully it made my ear ring.

I mumbled, "Drew Smyth-Sommers and Teri Baxter."

"Thank you very much. Be at the Church Street station tomorrow morning at ten sharp to make a formal statement. If you're not on time, I'm going to put out an APB on you and have you arrested." He hung up.

What is it about O'Connor that automatically makes my hackles rise?

We have a strange relationship. We disagree on almost every topic. He is arrogant, racist, and intolerant; he thinks I'm aggressive, bitchy, and too liberal. Every election found us screaming at each at the top of our lungs, our respective spouses valiantly trying to steer all conversations away from politics. And yet put us in a kitchen…

O'Connor loves to cook and eat as much as I do. We'd talk for hours about where to buy the best vegetables, what did we like better, Thai or Italian, argue endlessly (but amicably) about who makes the best bread in town (I like Grace Baking, he favors ACME), stuff like that. We cooked extravagant meals together, roasting whole pigs on a spit or making five-foot-high croquenbuches. But outside the kitchen it's war. Unless we're discussing, making, or eating food, we're like oil and water.

Our little exchange really woke me up. The hangover had dissipated and my stomach was howling from hunger. I was in the middle of eating an omelet when Jim called. No surprise there. His ex-wife discovering a body would make the rounds quickly. I let the machine run its course. I had no intention of answering it.

I imagined Jim clutching the phone, for once his benign, elfish face without a smile on it. One of the things I resent most about our divorce is that I no longer have Jim's riotous sense of humor to balance my cynical view of life. The Type B that took the edge off my Type A. He has a smile and that peculiarly Irish way of having a funny story on tap for every occasion. He and O'Connor made a good team, Jim the good cop to O'Connor's bad cop. I remembered O'Connor's wooden reply when he told me Jim had transferred to I.A. O'Connor's as dour and cynical as I am; maybe he needs Jim's joie de vivre as much as I do.

"Mary, I just talked to O'Connor and he told me you found a body at the restaurant. He didn't have time to tell me many details. My God, what's going on?"

He sounded unfairly proprietary, as if my concerns were still his goddamn concerns. I bet he was calling from work. Making calls to the ex sounding like he actually cared wouldn't go over well with wife number two.

"Mary, are you there? Please pick up the phone."

I picked up the phone.

"What do you want, Jim?"

"Mary, what in the hell happened? O'Connor called me from the restaurant."

"I went to work, found a body concealed in a laundry bag, called 911, end of story," I said flatly. I threw my half-eaten omelet into the garbage. I wasn't hungry anymore.

"Who was it? An employee?"

"Jim, I've already played twenty questions with O'Connor and my mother. I really don't want to go through it a third time. I'm all right. Go back to work. Anyway, isn't this out of your jurisdiction now? I understand from O'Connor that you bailed on him, too. Internal Affairs, what a joke. You, one of the best homicide inspectors on the force, working for I.A."

In theory cops watching over cops is a good idea. In reality, it's the fanatically ambitious, the power mongers, the misfits who can't find partners to work with them that populate I.A.

"Do you think you could talk to me for five minutes without being sarcastic or nasty? I called because I'm worried about you.

Anyway, I'm not at work. Tina and the kids are visiting her mother for a week. And for your information, I didn't bail on O'Connor. He understood my decision. The hours were too much. Tina and the kids need me."

I whispered into the phone, "Need you? I need you."

"No, Mary, you don't." He sounded exasperated. We'd had this argument many times before. The twentieth time around didn't make it any easier to hear. "Tina's here when I am, not off baking two thousand pies for assholes who could care less." His voice got louder and angrier with each word. My own anger began escalating in response to his, and my free hand grabbed my stomach. Those evil crunchies started roiling and churning. I felt like I was going to be sick again.

"Is that how I failed you?" I shouted back. "I didn't stay at home merrily raising children and fighting the constant mold on the walls that comes from living in that foggy hellhole you call the Sunset?"

I slammed down the phone.

The phone rang several times, but the caller didn't leave a message.

Chapter 5

The last year of our marriage had been ugly. We'd reached the stage where the simplest response was automatically interpreted as a Fuck You. In a classic case of denial, I told myself over and over again it'd get better if only I'd keep my mouth shut. Two years ago, reality reared its ugly head at three o'clock in the morning on a New Year's Eve that was so cold I broke my key in the lock of the car door and had to use the spare hidden under my car fender.

After attempting to enter the house without making a sound, I'd tripped over a dark mountain of moving boxes neatly stacked in the foyer. I turned on the light. Eight boxes sat lined up in two neat rows, one row stacked on top of the other, his treasure trove of old jazz LPs on the bottom, shirts, shoes, and sweaters on top. In Catholic school cursive, he had written the contents on the side of each box, plus his name: McCreary, 425 Magnolia Street, San Francisco. He'd even added the zip code.

Jim lay in our bed, the faint light from the foyer outlining the long, slim silhouette of his body propped up against the pillows.

"And a Happy New Year to you, too."

"I'm sorry, Mary. I wish it didn't have to be this way."

"I just finished an eighteen-hour shift. Couldn't you have picked a more opportune evening?" Exhaustion saturated every pore in my body. On the verge of physical collapse, I gripped the footboard of the bed for support.

He turned on his bedside lamp. He was fully clothed, even to the point of having his jacket on. The hot white light from the lamp bleached out his freckles and gave him a sickroom pallor.

"Does it matter, Mary? When aren't you working an extra shift or overtime?" He sounded as tired as I felt.

"It's what I do, Jim," I protested. "Just like you're a cop."

"No, it's more than that for you. I'm not the most important thing in your life. I'm not even a close second. First your job, then your mother and sister, and I come in third."

"That's not true," I cried.

"It doesn't matter whether you think it's true. *I* think it's true," he said, pointing a finger at his chest.

"It's the baby thing, isn't it?" I accused.

Jim and I had been to a parade of fertility specialists in the last two years, but with no success.

In slow motion, he eased himself off of the bed and walked across the room to the doorway. I twisted around, my body groaning with the effort, my heart breaking with the certainty that he was walking out that door.

"No, Mary, I wish it were that simple. I'm leaving now. You probably don't believe me, but I do still love you in a way. And I know you love me." He paused. "But not enough."

My arms out-stretched in supplication, I begged, "Don't leave, Jim. I'll quit, do something else. I'll…"

"No," he interrupted in a voice so quiet I barely heard him. "You love what you do. How happy do you think we'll be if you quit? It won't work. I've got to go."

My arms fell limp at my sides, my throat dry with fear. What in the hell was happening?

"Where are you going?"

He straightened up, as if bracing himself for a blow. Of course, it should have been me bucking up for the hit.

"Tina Regan's."

As if struck by lightning, every hair on my body stood on end. If I had thought about it, I guess I would've assumed he was going to one of his brothers' houses.

"Tina Regan, Tina Regan," I repeated. "Isn't she the woman whose husband, the motorcycle cop, was killed last year by some motorist hyped on meth?"

He nodded.

"You mean the widow with four children?" I was incredulous. "It's her kids, isn't it?"

It had never occurred to me he might leave me for another woman, the ultimate punch in the gut. Literally. The more he talked, the more my stomach twisted itself in a pretzel.

"It's not her kids. She's a nice, soft sort of woman."

"That's what you say about quilted toilet paper, not people."

"I can always count on you to have a smart, bitchy remark handy." He closed his eyes. His eyelids fluttered slightly, like he was trying to control himself.

"No insults, okay? I don't want to remember you like this. I want the nice memories." His hand moved toward me as if to touch my cheek and then stopped. "You're beautiful, smart, funny, sexy, but you know." He inhaled like it was the last breath of air in the room and then let it all out. "You're not easy. At this point in my life I want easy. And I won't play third fiddle anymore. I'm sorry."

He lingered in the doorway. I took a mental snapshot for posterity; his eyes the color of forget-me-nots, the deeply etched laugh lines around his mouth and eyes, and the curve of his long, shapely fingers gripping the door jamb. Then he was gone.

I grabbed a lapel of my chef's jacket and ripped—hard. The buttons popped off and scattered, click, click, click on the hardwood floor. Hail began pelting the windows and roof; its clatter drowned out my high-pitched weeping and the thud of the front door slamming.

I knew I'd go crazy if I didn't stop replaying that scene in my head. I paced around the house like a tiger looking for fresh kill, searching for anything to distract me until I was ready for bed. I picked up books only to throw them down after reading a few paragraphs, did some laundry, tried to watch television but switched it off in disgust as every show seemed to be geared to twenty-two-year-olds. Finally around midnight I thought I might be tired enough for bed. I slept on the living room couch so I couldn't hear the click of the answering machine in case he called back. I tossed and turned for several hours until eventually I fell asleep around four in the morning. Despite my exhaustion, severe hunger pangs woke me up at seven. Not surprising. Since I lost my breakfast on the floor of the laundry closet, yesterday's food intake consisted of half an omelet and eight ounces of brandy. And lots of coffee.

I needed food.

I took a hot shower to melt away the couch-induced kinks in my neck, threw on some clothes, and was heading out the door to the local diner for breakfast when Amos appeared at my front steps with a dozen donuts in hand.

"Hey, girlfriend. Need some processed sugar in your life?"

Amos Savage is my best friend and second-in-command at the restaurant. When Jim left, he moved in with me for three months to make sure I bathed and ate.

"You're a life saver." I gave him a hug.

I love low-down junk food. Not fast food, but hot dogs from Casper's, hot out of the deep-fat fryer doughnuts, anything bound to up your cholesterol level over three hundred. Those burgers smothered in mayo and grease from the old Clown Alley on Columbus. Thank God it closed down some years ago—a few hundred more of those and I'd be staring a major heart attack in the face by the age of thirty-five.

Once in the kitchen I did my thing with the espresso machine and Amos set the table, his long elegant fingers rummaging around in my dining room for linen napkins and silver napkin rings. We'd known each other for over five years, and his overwhelming physical grace still stops me in my tracks every now and then. He'd been a dancer with Alvin Ailey before a knee injury sidelined him forever, but he still moved as if he were on stage. Watching him arrange a dessert plate was like being at a performance of *Swan Lake*, every movement perfect and sure. I'm in awe of people with that sort of grace. My clumsiness as a child and teenager is a family legend. All the ease I've developed in the kitchen is because of hard work and training.

"I called you five times this morning. I even tried the cell phone. What gives?"

I snapped my fingers.

"Thanks for reminding me. I'd better turn on my cell phone in case my mother needs to get a hold of me. Jim and I had a fight last night and he kept calling back. I turned everything off and slept in the living room."

"The newspaper ain't saying nothin'. I got ten calls from people asking me where in the hell you were. Everybody and their mother is trying to reach you to get the skinny."

I bet. Every chef I knew was probably gagging with curiosity. And it's not people being ghoulish.

Even in a big town like San Francisco, the hard-core cooking community is relatively small. People move around a lot to learn from other chefs, so you get to know people in the field. Because our hours are so strange, the demands relentless, and the stress unforgiving, we share a strange world that glues us together in a type of camaraderie that's probably only shared by theater folk. Food's a lot like theater. We have to dance on cue. Otherwise your food's cold, or the wine doesn't taste good with your food, or you're missing your fork, or the piecrust on your dessert has the consistency of a floury hockey puck.

We raised our voices over the hissing of the espresso machine.

"If I may say so, you look like shit, honey. Why don't you go back to bed?"

"Got to go downtown to make a statement." I handed him a latte and we sat down.

The doughnuts were arranged on an antique china platter in a neat little pyramid, topped with a donut hole. It was worthy of a photo in *Gourmet*.

"I bet—" I took a big bite of a chocolate old-fashioned. "It was—" another bite—"Thom."

Amos stopped mid-chew; the powdered sugar on his jelly doughnut mustached his upper lip like a dusting of snow on a coal heap.

"Yeah, like he and Carlos were bosom buddies. Went bar hopping together, picked up chicks," he snorted. "The only 'chicks' Thom picks up are the chickens on Polk Street. Would you stop with this Thom-bashing? It's getting old."

I sulked for a few moments.

"You know what a pain in the ass he is. The way he sucks up to those rich socialites. It's disgusting."

He'd finished his jelly doughnut and was about to chomp into a maple bar.

"Get out of your ivory tower, girl. He forces you to create and stretch, otherwise you'd be pushing apple pie on everyone. And no rich-bitch socialite is going to pay ten dollars per person for apple pie."

"It's his fault that I discovered Carlos' body."

Amos looked at me with the scorn I deserved. I couldn't help it; there was something about the controller that rubbed me the wrong way.

Amos's watch went off. He got up, got a glass of water, and returned to the table to take his second round of pills for the day.

"How's the T-cell count these days?" I asked.

"I don't ask, they don't tell. I feel pretty good though. Thank the Lord," he intoned in his best Baptist bass. Amos comes from a small town in Alabama. His father is a hellfire-and-brimstone Baptist preacher who's convinced his son is possessed by the Devil. Amos told me there's only one thing worse than being black in a town like that and it's being gay. Well, if you're black and gay, you catch the first bus out of town.

"You look great and nothing's wrong with your appetite." His six-foot-four frame had filled out in the last year, erasing that gaunt, I'm-dying-from-AIDS look. The disease has taken its toll though. He's only thirty-three years old and his hair's as white as meringue. Partly because San Francisco is a gay mecca like New York, and partly because gays are attracted to the food scene, both men and women, the number of deaths from AIDS has been staggering. I've lost count of the number of men I've worked with who have died.

"I'm back at the gym five days a week. Ran into Thom there yesterday. Don't know why that guy's so fat. He works out more than I do."

"I know why," I grumbled. "He eats like a pig. He's always begging desserts off me."

"Well, Brent must be paying him a mighty fine salary. He was driving a brand-new red BMW. And not a puny little boxy number, no ma'am, but one of those sleek roadsters."

I stopped eating and looked at him in amazement. "Those cars cost at minimum thirty grand. How could he possibly afford a car like that?"

"Maybe he's got a rich sugar daddy somewheres."

Memo to self: ask Brent for a raise.

He reached for the second to the last doughnut. I slapped his hand.

"Stop, I want to take those on the road with me. I might get hungry later on."

"Okay, you need it more than I do. You're too skinny. Your tits and ass done packed their bags and left town." I resisted the impulse look down and check my ever-shrinking cleavage. "I got to go to a meetin' anyway. Missed the last couple of days."

The food business is rife with drug and alcohol abuse. You never hear about this in the Wednesday food section of the *San Francisco Chronicle*. The general public thinks that a chef's life is glamorous, creating wonderful little meals for celebrities. Well, in addition to cooking scrumptious tidbits for the beautiful people, we also produce two hundred dinners a night for the rest of humanity. This entails a lot of hard work and overtime. Sometimes it's almost impossible to generate the energy you need to start your shift, and after your shift, when you want to wind down, you're too wound up to even sit still. This is where the drugs and alcohol come in; you take something to get up and take something to get down, it's a vicious cycle. Many people are in recovery for both alcohol and drug abuse.

Being married to Jim probably saved me from chronic alcoholism. While alcohol is no stranger to any Irish household, Jim was so pathetically square that I had a safe respite from the crazy, adrenaline-junkie world of cooking whenever I walked in my front door. I have that edgy sort of personality that all too easily sees booze as a convenient and welcome form of self-medication. The tendency to bitchiness disappears when I've had a few. I become wonderfully indulgent, even, God forbid, happy-go-lucky. The transition from Cruella de Ville to Snow White in just two shakes of a cocktail shaker frightens me. I wonder who is the real Mary Ryan? I made an ironclad rule when Jim left that I would not, under any circumstances, drink alone.

I shooed Amos on his way, promising I'd fill him in on the gory details once I got the okay from O'Connor.

I was inserting the key in the ignition when my cell phone rang.

"Hope you're dressed, Ryan. By my calculations you should be on the bridge by now."

O'Connor.

"If I didn't have to talk to obnoxious cops all the time I'd be on the bridge by now."

"There are no obnoxious cops, just obnoxious witnesses. I called to tell you I'm not going to be at the station. Sergeant Lee will take your statement."

Asshole. Yesterday, he reads me this riot act and now he doesn't have the courtesy to make an appearance.

"Did you get any sleep? You looked pretty whacked out yesterday."

"No. Jim and I got into an ugly fight and…Wait a minute… Are you checking up on me? I can take care of myself." I jabbed the end button and hurled the cell phone over my shoulder into the back seat.

All the well-being built up by some espresso and excellent doughnuts dissipated. Self-destructive I know, but I replayed the telephone call with Jim the entire length of the bridge. Suddenly, I found myself parked at the Church Street station lot with no recollection of the entire trip.

I half expected to see Jim lurking around the hallways. Considering my state of mind, I might have committed murder myself if he'd tried to confront me. I gave my statement to a sergeant who had been at the scene and was out of there in little over an hour.

I figured I'd better go to the restaurant and find out what the game plan was. Maybe Juan had tried to reach me. I had no idea when we were re-opening. Tuesday's opera night, and the restaurant would have been booked for months. Brent was probably on the phone to the mayor right now, pulling every political and media string he possessed to make sure we opened on Tuesday. No doubt on Wednesday morning there would be beaucoup references to American Fare in the society section of the *Chron*. To ensure our preeminence as the dining room of S.F.'s rich and famous, Brent might even go so far as to have himself photographed in his chef's whites, with the most august of S.F. society's elite hanging off his arm. The society page would probably refer to Carlos' death as an "incident," if at all.

Carlos' death was more than just an incident with me. I'd talk to Brent about setting up some sort of fund for Carlos' wife. It was the least we could do. Poor guy. What in the hell was he mixed up in?

Chapter 6

I arrived at the restaurant at noon. The crime-scene tape was gone and a delivery truck was parked in front filled with cases of wine. I maneuvered my wagon behind the truck and walked through the dining room.

A dining room, no matter how extravagant the lighting or decor, always looks forlorn without customers. It's like a theater waiting for its audience. The maître d' is like the usher, bringing you to your table and handing you a program in the form of a menu. Think of tablecloths, silverware, and wineglasses as stage props. Act One is the unfurling of the napkin, the reading of the menu, the clink of wineglasses as you toast each other.

Act Two is the meal itself. The lead actor, the chef, has perfected the part by creating a meal that should surprise and satiate you. Like an actor, a chef sets out to woo you so that you'll come back again and again. Unlike the theater, where the audience is by and large passive, the diner plays a critical part. The meal should be composed not only of good food but also good conversation. A meal is not complete without fine repartee, whether it be a heated discussion of that day's headlines or saucy bantering back and forth between two people heady with wine and potential romance.

Act Three is dessert, the denouement, where the last bite should sum up your meal, your conversation. It's the amen. That's why I'm a pastry chef. I get the last word.

When I entered the kitchen, Juan, the maître d', was leaning up against one of the long stainless steel tables, his body in that slack posture of lost thought. He and Brent met many years ago in Denver. Juan started as a dishwasher, graduated to pantry chef, then to the line. Although he was talented enough to be a chef somewhere in his own right, he veered off into wines. Through sheer determination and hard work he is now one of the best sommeliers in the city. He introduced Chilean and Australian wines into the restaurant scene and cultivated a number of South American wineries that bottle exclusively for us.

Juan's one of the few Hispanics in the restaurant biz who's broken through the glass ceiling. Although we've never developed the bond Brent and I have, we respect each other and work well together. I rely on him heavily as my Spanish is limited to *Hola* and *Como esta?*

I coughed a couple of times to let him know I was there. He jerked around, his face ashen. Relentlessly anal about his appearance, today he wore a white polo shirt stained with coffee, and his jet-black hair, normally slicked back close to his head like a seal, was rumpled.

Juan walked up to me, his voice distracted. "Good morning, Mary. I see you did not get my message. Brent decided to close the restaurant over the weekend. We will open for dinner on Tuesday. I anticipate being very busy. People are curious, you know, like vultures feeding on carrion."

"Wow, I'm impressed," I said. "Did you clean this up all by yourself? It was a disaster yesterday."

The kitchen was spotless once more. The stainless steel tables, shiny and smart, had been scrubbed clean of print powder and all the coffee cups had been collected and washed. All traces of S.F.P.D. were gone. The only hint that a murder had taken place was a strip of yellow crime-scene tape with big black letters that said "DO NOT CROSS S.F.PD." that had been crisscrossed over the entrance to the corridor where the laundry room was.

"A couple of the guys helped me. Unfortunately, the laundry closet is still off limits." He flicked his wrist in the direction of the laundry closet. "They told me it would be cleared for us to use by Monday. *Madre de Dios*, those cops are complete pigs," he said in disgust. He must have caught his reflection in the sheen of the stainless steel table because he ran both hands through his hair trying to slick it back down in an attempt to correct his uncharacteristic dishabille. "You would not believe it. I found coffee cups everywhere, cigarette butts ground into the tile floor. Someone even walked off with the cooking wine."

"How long did they keep everyone?"

"Oh, for hours, Mary. I didn't get home until at least four that afternoon. Poor Carlos. I talked with his wife this morning. She is very upset. She had to identify the body."

"It was…pretty awful." I tried, but failed, to block out an image of Carlos' battered face. "He was strangled and very badly beaten."

Juan leaned toward me and gently cupped my chin in his hand for a brief moment, his face creased with concern. "Why don't you go home and get some rest. If I may say so, you look very tired. I'll call you if anything comes up."

"Thanks, I think I'll take your advice. Is Brent here?" I hadn't seen any evidence of anyone else, but Brent might be upstairs in the office mending fences with Mrs. Gerson.

"No. He is still distraught about what happened last night. He decided not to come in today. If he calls I will let him know you asked about him."

As he talked his hands made small flourishes in the air. The affectations were resurfacing; I could leave without feeling guilty. Placing a firm hand on the small of my back, he steered me out the kitchen.

"I'll talk to you later. Bye," I said over my shoulder as I entered the dining room.

A second too late I saw out of the corner of my eye the delivery guy barreling toward me. He didn't see me because the dolly was stacked up to the top with cases of wine. Before I could jump out of his way, he ran right into me. I screamed blue murder as the edge of the dolly sliced into my shin.

"Mary?" Juan came running from back of the kitchen.

Seeing me clutching my shin and moaning from the pain, Juan began screaming Spanish invectives at the delivery guy; his rage was terrifying. God knows what he said, but it must have been horrendous. The deliveryman shrank in fear, his back bending over a table in an attempt to get away from Juan's fury.

I limped over to Juan and put my hand on his arm to stop him. He wheeled around and was about to cuff me when he realized at the last second who I was. He stopped just short of shattering my jaw. We stood there frozen for a few seconds as if in a movie still, his arm half lowered and my arm half raised against the blow I had expected.

Finally, Juan lowered his arm completely and apologized in his most courteous manner. "I am so sorry, Mary. I lost my temper. Please forgive me," he implored. "I was so angry that this imbecile barged into you. I was not thinking."

The delivery guy across from me silently mouthed what looked like Hail Marys.

"Well, don't just apologize to me, apologize to him. You scared the shit out of him, too," I managed to squeak out.

Juan turned toward the driver and said something softly in Spanish, then stuck out his hand. The driver shook it very gingerly, bowed his head, took the dolly of wine, and headed for the truck.

I had to get out of there fast. Blood was dripping down my shin from where the dolly hit me. If Juan saw me bleeding he'd insist on bandaging me up.

"Gotta go, I'll call tomorrow." I limped out of the restaurant as fast as I could, ignoring his offers of assistance.

What a bizarre scene. I'd never seen Juan lose it like that.

Running a restaurant is an endless day of stomping out fires. Your dishwasher shows up drunk and you can't find a replacement. The compressor on your refrigeration unit blows up on the hottest day of the year. Your best waiter decides to check into detox the night of the symphony opening. Juan deftly handled these sorts of crises without so much as incurring an extra crease in his pants. The stains on his shirt were as shocking as his uncharacteristic rage.

I sat in the car for ten minutes, trying to stem the bloody mess from my shin with some of the napkins I had brought with my doughnuts. I fashioned a bandage out of napkins and a couple of rubber bands, hoping it would hold until I got home.

I started the car and was about to pull away when I heard a horn beep. In the rearview mirror I saw a red BMW pull up behind me.

Thom.

I rolled down the window, but kept the engine running to let him know I wasn't going to give the encyclopedia version of yesterday's events. Even on his day off Thom was a walking advertisement for Ralph Lauren: khakis, white linen shirt, and tasseled loafers. His outfit probably cost more than the blue book of my car.

Thom usually sauntered everywhere, his lazy style in sharp contrast to most of us in the restaurant who operate at light speed. Today he actually sprinted over to my car.

"Mary, how are you? Did you see anything? Was it just too gory?"

I debated which question he really wanted answered. I wasn't about to go into details; he probably wanted salacious tidbits to bandy about the gym. "No blood, if that's what you mean."

"So lucky you didn't run into the murderer. Are you sure you didn't see anything? Did you sleep a wink last night? Is there anything I can do?"

These trilogies of questions were getting annoying. However, he was being awfully friendly. Stung by Amos's criticism, I was determined to be nice.

"No, I didn't get much sleep last night, but I'm all right. How about you? You look a little pale." Naturally florid, today he looked washed out, accenting the rigidity of the botox treatment.

"Surviving, just barely. Well, when I got Juan's message about the…" he paused, searching for the right word.

"Murder?" I chimed in.

"Yes, if you must put it like that. As soon as I got the message I ran over to Mrs. Gerson's and begged for forgiveness. I convinced her this was a blessing in disguise. If the benefit is held in the spring, the flowers would be so much more…well, spectacular."

I'm sure Carlos' wife didn't see her husband's murder in quite that light. I promised myself I'd be nicer to Thom in the future, but he was making things very difficult.

"I'm sure Mrs. Gerson was reason personified." My voice was dry as cooking parchment. I bet that harpy and Thom commiserated for hours about how Carlos' death had momentarily derailed her social climbing. Time to leave. If the conversation continued in this vein, I'd be up on charges for vehicular manslaughter. I revved the motor a little to let Thom know that our conversation was at an end. "See you later, Thom. We're opening on Tuesday for lunch. Check with Juan. He's inside."

Thom leaned over and placed a pudgy hand on the edge of window to make sure I didn't drive off. "Mary, wait. Did you go upstairs at all?"

A mean, salty wind from the bay was whipping through the Mission, yet Thom's forehead was beaded with sweat and the little silk scarf tied jauntily around his neck was damp around the edges.

"No, I was in the dining room or the kitchen the whole time. You look stressed. Is anything missing?"

"I don't think so. They called me last night with an inventory of the equipment in the office. It sounds like it's all there. I'm going in to double-check and phone the insurance company. That equipment is top of the line, sweetie. They'd better have kept their clumsy hands off my computer." His mouth puckered in distaste, as if the S.F.P.D. were lepers and their disease-crusted hands had spread life-threatening germs all over his equipment. "I'll sue the department if those oafs so much as touched the keyboard."

Once he said oafs, all bets were off.

"You know, Thom." This time I pronounced the "th" on purpose. "My ex-husband's a cop. The detective in charge of this case is a personal friend of mine. I wouldn't go broadcasting your low opinions of S.F.P.D. too loudly."

When I mispronounced his name he flinched, stood up straight, sucked in his gut, and shot me a look of pure hatred. "Bitch," he spat. "Too bad there wasn't room for two in that laundry bag." He turned heel and stomped into the restaurant as fast as his tasseled loafers could carry him.

Driving across the whole length of the bridge I obsessed on Carlos' murder and forced myself to answer some very basic questions.

If you died next week, would you want to have wasted what precious time you had left hating your ex-husband? That was a toughie. I moved on to an easier one.

If you died next week, would you want to have spent your last few days in a house painted instant-depression mauve? But, do you have the energy to paint? The first answer was obviously no. Unfortunately, the second answer was another no. Impasse.

I drove straight to my local hardware store and whiled away an hour looking at paint chips. It was the first time in eight months I was doing something that wasn't food-related.

I asked the guy behind the counter, "How many gallons of latex will it take to cover up this yucky mauve color on my living room walls?"

I'd reached the stage in my life when I was older than most of the people who waited on me. I resent the way that when you turn thirty, not only are you not cool, you're invisible, too. This guy was no exception. Plus, he had four piercings I could see and God knows how many I couldn't. And his hair was dirty to boot. I try not to make value judgments on this sort of stuff, but it's hard. If this guy had bothered to make eye contact instead of moving his eyes somewhere in my direction, I might have been more tolerant.

"How big a space we talking about?" He was chewing gum and talking at the same time. The gum kept getting caught on the stud in his tongue. I felt my stomach flip-flop.

Trying to avoid his various piercings, I fixed on a pimple above his right eyebrow.

"Standard living room size. This mauve's pretty intense though."

"Usually a couple of gallons, but for your house…who knows? We don't do house calls, lady."

I hate being called "lady." Giving him one of my "you jerk" looks, I scooped up all my paint chips and left the store.

As I was walking to my car, I saw a young Latino male standing behind a lamppost.

Oh, my God, it was Gilberto, Carlos' brother.

I rushed up to him and was about to hug him when I stopped dead. He didn't move to greet me, his body was stiff, his eyes fierce.

"You're the one who found Carlitos."

It wasn't a question.

I moved to touch him. He flinched. I backed off.

"He's dead."

Again, it wasn't a question.

"Yes, Gilberto. I'm so sorry. I…is there anything I can do?"

His face paled, and then contorted with grief as he tried not to cry. He opened his mouth several times as if to speak, then turned away from me and ran across three lanes of traffic.

He was out of sight within thirty seconds. I screamed, "Wait," several times to no avail. He must have tailed me all the way from the restaurant. Why didn't he go to the police to get information about Carlos?

Knowing Gilberto had followed me all the way from San Francisco without my having a clue was pretty unsettling. By the time I reached my block, I'd convinced myself into near hysterics that the blue van trailing three cars behind me all the way from the paint store to my house was after me. I couldn't get a good look at the driver; the windows were darkened. But when I parked a couple of doors away from my house, it continued down the street. In my neighborhood it was probably filled with screaming toddlers and a harassed suburban mom driving home from the grocery store. It was just my overactive imagination. The events of the last two days were making me paranoid.

I changed before the inevitable inquisition with my mother that afternoon. The clothes I'd worn yesterday were in a sad pile on my bedroom floor. I threw them away knowing every time I put them on, I'd think about Carlos' battered face in the laundry bag.

Chapter 7

My mother and stepfather, Ed, live on a cul-de-sac in Kensington, a wooded enclave in the hills between Berkeley and El Cerrito. My mother has either a trowel or a knitting needle in hand, weather depending. Ed's a great reader, with a keen interest in politics.

One of my nicest memories is sitting around the kitchen table discussing history with him, especially WWII. He was a radio operator with the Royal Air Force and was captured by the Japanese early on in the war. Ed spent four years in a Japanese POW camp. That man has some stories to tell. His latest hobby is shortwave radio. He beeps and dots by the hour.

I spent a couple of hours at their kitchen table reliving the murder several times over. Once Ed heard the most salient details and ascertained I was all right, he went back to beeping and dotting, knowing my mother would retell the mostly grisly bits at dinner that night.

As I sat in my mother's kitchen, listening to the gurgle of the garden fountain through the open door and watching my mother scatter walnuts throughout the garden for the squirrels, the ball of pain lodged between my shoulder blades since the morning of the murder gradually disappeared. My equilibrium was returning. Peace.

Once the squirrels had been fed, the two of us sat at the kitchen table guzzling more coffee and thumbing through the mountains of catalogues she'd gotten in the mail in anticipation of Christmas sales.

"Mom, look. Truly hideous," I chuckled, pointing to a gaudy, sequined number that had trailer trash written all over it. "And they want three hundred dollars for it."

"Mary, I talked to Jim this morning."

The pain came roaring back with a speed and ferocity that left me breathless. I looked at her in astonishment. Traitor, my inner voice screamed. Avoiding eye contact, she began flipping rapidly through a catalogue whose specialty was matching outfits for pets and their owners.

"Did he tell you about our fight? How I almost had a stroke over AT&T?" I demanded.

"No, we didn't talk about your fight. I still don't understand what happened between you two, but I don't think it's as simple as you make it out to be. That's another subject," she said firmly and slapped the catalogue closed.

Taking my hand that lay on the table, she squeezed it tight and looked right at me. "The person I love is you, and I'll do anything it takes to keep you safe. If that means talking to Jim, then I'll talk to Jim. Anyway, he called me, I didn't call him. So get that look off your face. He's worried about your safety. He wants you to stay with me until this case is solved."

Maybe spending the last week of my life hating my ex-husband was a good thing.

"Mom, I appreciate your concern, but I'm fine. Carlos' murder has nothing to do with me. I happened to stumble on his body. End of story. I resent Jim calling you up and getting you all worried. Besides, O'Connor's on the case. He wouldn't dare risk your wrath if anything happened to me. True?"

She nodded her head slowly. "I'd feel better if you were here."

"Look, I need to do a few things around the house. I can't stay here. Okay?" I squeezed her hand back. "I'm not answering my phone right now, I don't want to talk to him. If you want to talk to me, call once, then hang up and call again."

She acquiesced reluctantly. Jim knew what a worrywart my mother was. What in the hell was his problem?

When I finally got home it was after five and I was famished. No food in the house, of course. My stomach screamed in agony from tea burns and starvation.

Although chefs cook with all sorts of wonderful ingredients all day long and conjure up mouthwatering culinary extravaganzas for other people, if they don't have families to feed, their cupboards at home are often bare because when do they have time to shop? The only staples I always have on hand are sugar, flour, yeast, eggs, and salt, so I can always make bread. Otherwise I buy for events like dinner parties and barbeques. My cupboards are filled with things like capers and candied ginger, but no real food, as I eat at the restaurant. I know one chef who doesn't even have cutlery or dishes. He has one spoon and one coffee mug ready for use, if by chance he remembers to buy instant coffee.

The sole contents of my refrigerator were one moldy container of Kalamata olives, some Parmigiano-Reggiano, the heels of a stale loaf of Grace's Stormy baguette, a jar of Grey Poupon, and three pounds of Peet's coffee. Pathetic. I scraped the mold off the olives, mashed them up with a little of the Parmesan and the mustard, and toasted the bread. It wasn't half bad. As I munched down this culinary delight, the phone rang. Silence. Then the phone rang again. Sigh. Mom calling to make sure I got home in one piece.

"Mom, I'm fine."

"Is this Mary Ryan?" The voice was tentative and small.

"Uh, yeah. Who's this?"

"It's Teri from the restaurant. I really need to talk with you. Um, about Brent." She sounded extremely upset, her voice breathy and clipped like she was trying not to cry.

Teri Baxter, a bus person at the restaurant, was one of Brent's current squeezes. There are two kinds of redheads: the type with the rice paper-white skin and copper-gold hair, and Teri's type, the kind with skin the color of a peeled potato and hair so red that it looks like your finger would blister if you touched it. I'd never understood Brent's attraction to her.

Teri had worked at the restaurant for about six months. When she first started she made timid hints to me that what she really wanted to do was learn pastry. Normally, I love teaching and feel strongly about promoting from within. These days I just didn't want to explain why bread flour was different from pastry flour, what a "turn" in croissant dough was, why you had to temper eggs before you added them to hot milk, and so on. To her credit, she hadn't used her relationship with Brent to muscle her way in. She was a nice kid, much too nice to be mixed up with that hound Brent.

As I struggled to balance the phone on my ear and eat at the same time, I dropped the interior of my sandwich first down my shirt, then onto the floor. Shit. Mustard and black olives on white tee shirt, a winning combination.

"What's up?" I snapped, not so much at her as at my own clumsiness.

"Mary, I need to talk to you right away. The police were just here. I pretended I wasn't home. I didn't know what to say. With your ex-husband being a cop, I thought you might know what I should do."

To my tremendous embarrassment, the girl began to cry.

"Hey, everything's going to be okay. Calm down. It's procedure."

While she sobbed for a minute or two longer, I gathered up the olive bits that had fallen onto the floor and put them back in the sandwich.

Pulling herself together she sniffled, "You don't understand. Last night Brent called me and told me I shouldn't say anything about m...m...my relationship with him or anything about the restaurant. That they were going to try to embarrass him cause he's a big-name chef and he didn't want me to get dragged into anything. You know, for my sake."

I ignored the bullshit about his noble bid to save Teri's honor from the police. He didn't give a rat's ass about her potential humiliation. I honed in on the part I found interesting.

"So...what sort of things about the restaurant aren't you suppose to talk about?" I tried to make my voice sound casual, but I must have blown it because she hung up.

I called her back every ten minutes, but she wouldn't answer the phone. What game was Brent playing? After an hour of cooling my heels by the telephone, I reviewed my options. Do I go to the restaurant, find out where she lives, and then beat her door down demanding an explanation?

No, go to the source, I reasoned. I called Brent's house for the next half hour. Busy signal. By now my curiosity overwhelmed my exhaustion and I was getting a second wind. Time to drive over to that weasel Brent's house and find out the truth for myself. It might be something fairly innocent, but now I was intrigued. Brent could hang up on me, but he couldn't avoid me if I was on his doorstep.

I drove across the bridge for the second time that day and headed toward Brent's house in the city. I kept flicking my eyes to the rearview mirror, trying to see if there was a blue van behind me. Once or twice I thought I saw it, but reasoned that there must be hundreds of blue Plymouth vans. At one point it was the most popular van in the U.S.

There's no easy way to get anywhere in San Francisco these days. Most of the freeway's on-ramps and off-ramps were destroyed during the Loma Prieta earthquake. Due to neighborhood politics versus Caltrans versus the mayor's office versus the S.F. Board of Supervisors, the majority of these ramps were torn down and not replaced. One year after the Northridge earthquake, all Los Angeles freeway overpasses and ramps were operational. Ten years after Loma Prieta, Caltrans reopened the Cypress structure. Sometimes there's a heavy price for living in the land of the politically correct. On the plus side, the Embarcadero freeway was torn down and the waterfront now has a spectacular esplanade. The negative? It's impossible to get to the neighborhoods without using city streets.

After hitting every stoplight on Sloat, I finally reached St. Francis Woods where Brent lives, a precursor to the planned community. Back in the nineteen twenties, a developer created an exclusive section of elegant houses for San Francisco's well-to-do. The truly wealthy live in Pacific Heights, but St. Francis Woods has a firm understated refinement that declares this is where the real San Franciscans live. The houses are large and graceful, with tasteful paint jobs complemented by meticulously manicured yards. Late-model Jeeps or Rovers sit in the driveways. Today's version of June and Ward Cleaver country.

I rang the bell several times. I was so engrossed in my residual road rage that it was a minute before I realized there was a horrific argument going on inside. A man and a woman were yelling in Spanish at each other loud enough to drown out the delicate chime of the doorbell.

Tiptoeing my way through a flowerbed, I peeked through the living room window. Brent and Sharon were going at it hammer and tongs, no kids in sight. I knew that Brent was fluent in Spanish; it plays a not insignificant role in his ability to run a kitchen well: ninety percent of his staff is Latino. That his wife, Sharon, was equally fluent surprised me. I bet they were screaming at each other in Spanish in the naïve belief that the kids wouldn't understand them. Ha. The vitriol being flung back and forth in their living room was universal in any language.

The yelling got louder, the hand gestures more violent. Well, I thought, now is not the time to interrogate Brent. I'll make an exit and phone him in the morning. But then Sharon became so enraged she started throwing pillows at him. When she reached for a lamp, I started frantically banging my fists on the window in an effort to stop someone from getting hurt.

"Hey," I yelled as loud as I could. "No, Sharon, no!"

They both looked up and stopped their screaming. She asked him something in Spanish. He shook his head no.

Shooting me a look that would curdle milk, she put the lamp down and lumbered out of the room.

Brent opened the door, blocking the entrance with that solid Teutonic body of his. He'd obviously been crying, his face splotchy and mottled, his eyes as red as raw hamburger. Standing there mutely, he waited for me to make the first move. I felt like a complete jerk, but I'd come all this way and damned if I was going to leave empty-handed.

Maybe I'll just ease into the thing with Teri I thought. Making no comment regarding the fight I'd just witnessed, I said, "Brent, I was in the neighborhood and was wondering if you know when and where is Carlos' funeral?"

Brent stared at me as if I were speaking Martian. The inappropriateness of the question was blindly apparent, but I pressed on.

"I know this is a bad time"—his face said "No shit, Sherlock"—"but I'm kind of not answering my phone these days. And, uh, my answering machine seems to be on the fritz. Do you know?"

He rubbed his large hands over his face for a minute, probably hoping that when he removed his hands I'd mercifully be gone.

"Mary, call Juan. He'll know. I think he'll be at the restaurant tomorrow sometime. Just keep trying. I can't help you tonight."

He started to close the door. I needed to do something fast or I'd have made this trip for nothing. I quickly put my shoulder against the door so he couldn't close it.

"Uh, one more thing, Brent. I need to talk with you about something else. Can I come in, please?"

"Christ, Mary. Not now," Brent groaned.

I looked over Brent's shoulder to see if Sharon was anywhere in sight.

"I know it's not a good time, but I just talked to Teri Baxter, and she…"

Brent's face immediately flushed tomato red at the mention of her name. He dug five meaty fingers into my shoulder and pushed his face toward me, not three inches from mine, his breath hot on my cheeks. "This is none of your goddam business." He dug his fingers in further, just in case I didn't understand the first time, let go with a push, and then slammed the door shut.

I was still leaning lightly against the door, so that the force of it propelled me off the steps and down the front path. I went splat on the bricks. I was lucky I didn't break an ankle. Before I could get back on my feet, he closed the drapes and turned off the porch light, leaving me in the dark. I went to my car and sat there for a couple of minutes thinking about my next move. Obviously Brent wasn't going to tell me what was going on. I'd have to pry it out of Teri. Her address would be at the restaurant.

The alley in front of the restaurant was deserted, not one lone curious thrill seeker. American Fare is located near South Park. People told Brent he was crazy to open a large bistro-type restaurant in an area previously renowned for its S&M leather bars, but with Brent's unusual ability to nail trends, he predicted that the South Park area would become mecca to dot-com companies. For a song he bought a run-down, rat-infested brick building that used to be a meatpacking plant and transformed it into the West Coast's hottest restaurant. The collapse of the dot-com boom hadn't affected our bottom line yet, no doubt thanks to Brent's endless publicity gigs.

Big shivers climbed up and down my back when I got out of the car. Our proximity to the ocean and being sandwiched between old industrial warehouses makes the alley cold and damp. Even though it was dark, I decided to leave the lights off. I didn't want anyone to know I was here. I'd have trouble explaining why I was in the office when we were closed for the next three days.

I went through the kitchen, up the back staircase, and into the office. What the hell, I thought, and wrote down the other girlfriend's address too. I was just about to turn out the lights when voices wafted up the hallway. Someone was in the kitchen, and it sounded like they were coming up the stairs. I made a dive for Juan's desk and scrunched myself into the chair space.

When they entered the office, I recognized the voices immediately—Brent and Sharon. They must have left five minutes after I did.

Sharon said in a sharp voice, "What's the light doing on in here?"

"How should I know, Sharon? Maybe the police or Juan left it on. Let's get out of here. This place gives me the creeps."

"Your pride and joy? Spare me. You sure as hell didn't mind spending eighty hours here last week."

"Shar, lay off for once," Brent pleaded.

"Lay off, I'll lay you off, you bastard. The computer. I want it taken care of tonight."

"I told you already, everything on the computer's been erased. See?"

I heard clicking as Brent's fingers played over the keyboard.

"What about the invoices? Did he shred them?"

"No, he can't. He promised me he'd doctor new invoices. We shipped it with other stuff so it wouldn't be noticed. Mary signs for a lot of stuff, and so does Thom. We bundled it with other shipments."

"You call him right now to make sure he's on it," she demanded.

Oh shit, I thought, the jig is up. He's going to come around the front of the desk to use the phone, and he'll see me sardined under this desk.

But he replied in that patronizing voice I'd only heard him use with his wife, "I've already spoken with him about it. He's working on it. Do you have any idea how many invoices there are?"

"Stop whining," she ordered. "What about the menu? Is it on the menu?"

"No," he replied sullenly. "Do you think we're total idiots?"

"You don't want to know what I think," she said. "Let's go."

They turned out the light and left the office.

I waited five minutes and then un-pretzeled myself from under the desk. This whole thing was getting weirder and weirder. Why would Brent need to steal files from his own restaurant? Clutching the addresses in my hand, I slowly and quietly made my way out of the building.

No blue van in sight.

Chapter 8

Teri Baxter lived in Albany. If I'd actually displayed some polite interest in her I'd have discovered she lived two blocks away from me on San Pablo Avenue in a ratty stucco apartment house right next door to a seedy bar called The Glow Worm. The kind of place with no windows—just a door—where the regulars line up at ten in the morning for their first shot. Her apartment building, a blank utilitarian style that was de rigueur in the sixties, screamed urban prison. Although I couldn't imagine living in a place like this, the reality is that at seven dollars an hour this is what Teri probably could afford, if she were willing to sacrifice charm for privacy.

Despite all the hype, the food business pays barely subsistence wages. A few big name chefs like Brent make a ton of dough, but the majority slog along until they realize they aren't going to make more than about twelve dollars an hour, usually no benefits. If you're lucky, you get a job in the hotels, which pay well and have benefits. I was fortunate. I'd hitched my star to Brent, who had parlayed his talents into a virtual culinary empire. My salary was decent, but I was in a tiny minority. In particularly bitter moments, I viewed restaurants as the late twentieth-century version of the sweatshop.

Standing before Teri's door, I heard the television blaring. I rang the doorbell and hollered, "Teri, it's me, Mary. Let me in."

No answer.

I shouted louder, "Teri, please let me in. I have to talk to you."

She opened the door. Her eyes raw from crying, she resembled one of those creepy all-white rabbits with the pink eyes. She sniffled something that sounded like "come in."

Teri's studio was so small she could easily brush her teeth at the sink in the bathroom with one hand and simultaneously fry eggs at the stove with the other. The furniture consisted of a nightstand, a queen-size bed, and several pieces of expensive media equipment. Her TV was wider than my kitchen table.

Dramatic music overwhelmed the tiny room. Automatically, we both turned toward the television. Heathcliff and Cathy were on the moors, the wind whipping around them.

Teri walked over to the VCR and turned it off, saying, "My favorite movie." She plopped down on the unmade bed, positioning herself between three remote controls and the remains of a bowl of popcorn.

"One of mine, too," I admitted.

There was no place to sit besides the bed because all the available space was devoted to her wide-screen television, CD player, tape deck, and VCR. I shifted my weight, trying to look nonthreatening.

My voice was gentle. "Teri, I spoke to Brent tonight." That part was true. "You can't protect him any longer. The police need to know everything. Anything might be important. I'm sure Brent had a very good reason for telling you to keep certain things from the police, but it's not in your best interest. You need to talk with them."

She started to cry again, her sobbing loud and sharp. I hated Brent. Here she was wrapped up in her dingy bedclothes, watching a movie about an impossible love affair, crying her eyes out, and eating microwave popcorn for dinner. I couldn't in my wildest nightmares compare Brent to Olivier, but obviously she felt she was living in a drama of Heathcliff/Cathy-like proportions.

I walked over to her bed and gently placed my hands on both her shoulders and said quietly, but forcefully, "Teri, stop crying. Stop." I took her chin in my hand and made her look at me.

Once we established eye contact, she started to pull herself together. She stood up. "Let me wash my face," she muttered thickly.

While she cleaned herself up, I checked out her apartment: tacky, tacky, tacky. The walls were painted that ubiquitous "sand" color apartment owners love, and aside from the all-consuming electronic equipment, there weren't any pictures on the walls, or plants, or anything that reflected Teri's personality. Even the bedclothes were nondescript, the same color as her walls. The only personal object in the room was a blurry picture of Brent sautéing over some burners propped up on her nightstand. He looked hot and tired, not very sexy.

Turning toward the kitchen I got the surprise of my life. She'd taken all the cupboard doors off her upper cabinets, and filled them with lovely Italian ceramic plates and platters, and Venetian glass goblets. An enormous ceramic platter propped up on a plate stand caught my eye. For years I'd drooled over that very platter in the windows of Biordi's in North Beach, but had never had the nerve to buy it. I walked over to one of the cupboards and took a heavy, cobalt blue Venetian goblet in my hand. Even in the glow from the cheap fluorescent light it was beautiful.

Teri came out of the bathroom and found me coveting her dishes. She looked a little less rabbitty.

"Isn't it just perfect? I make a point of buying one thing a month."

Embarrassed to be caught snooping in her cupboards, I made a show of filling one of those exquisite goblets with water from her sink, took a couple of perfunctory sips, and gently set it down on the Formica.

"I've been lusting after that platter for years," I confessed. "You have some beautiful things."

"Brent bought me that platter last month. Isn't it gorgeous? When he comes over, he cooks for me, and we pretend we're in Italy and have picnics on the bed." She smiled in remembrance.

For a brief second I pictured the two of them drinking frascati and eating figs wrapped with prosciutto, those gaily painted plates covering the ugly bedspread. I also understood why Brent had taken to her. She was simple and vulnerable and probably the one person in his life besides his children who just accepted him the way he was. He didn't have to be the trend-setting sexy chef or long-suffering husband, just plain old Brent Brown from Denver. And looking at her kitchen shelves lined with all that exquisite glassware and ceramics, I saw she obviously had a deeper, more sensual side. I bet she wore nondescript pastel clothing from Mervyn's over expensive black lacy demi-bras from Victoria's Secret.

"Teri, what did Brent ask you to say? Did he tell you to lie for him?"

Standing there hugging herself tight with her arms, she hedged, "Well, no, not exactly. He said the police would be asking questions about the night of, you know, the murder and they'd probably ask if he and I, were, well, you know, that sort of stuff. Then they might ask about the money and stuff."

Having scared her off once, I decided to lie. "Oh yeah, the money. Brent mentioned it to me a couple of months ago. What did he tell you?"

She sat down on the edge of the bed, nervously picking at the nubs on her blankets. "Well, one night when he came over and we'd had a lot to drink, Brent told me how in another couple of years he'd be on easy street. I asked him if the restaurant was doing well and he said the restaurant was doing fantastic. Then he raised his glass in the air and sloshed wine all over the bedclothes and started to giggle about how much money he was making on the side that nobody knew about. I guess he realized he'd said something he shouldn't because he got all worried looking. He told me never to tell a soul. And I haven't, not a single person. I swear." She sounded like she was making a Girl Scout pledge.

Hmm, maybe he was getting kickbacks from some of the purveyors. Pretty standard stuff. Times were tough, with unprecedented competition from abroad since the passage of NAFTA, especially from South America. The general public has no idea how much of their food stock comes from abroad. In the winter eighty percent of your fruit is from South America. Most likely the salmon you had for dinner was bred in a Chilean salmon farm. Even the South American wine industry is making some serious inroads on the American wine market. Despite the hefty tariffs the U.S. lays on these imports, these wines are available for next to nothing.

"So how much money, Teri? Five thousand a year, ten thousand a year?" I must have sounded impatient because she suddenly turned huffy and defensive.

"I don't know. But from what he said, I kinda thought it might be a lot."

I was so frustrated I wanted to break that beautiful platter of hers. Try as I might, I couldn't see how this could be big money. Most businesses I know run on razor-thin profit margins. They could slip Brent the odd hundred, but not the big money Brent had boasted about. Time to talk with Brent again.

"Teri, when are you going to see the police? You need to tell them about the money," I said, adding gently, "or I will."

"I know," she said, her voice high as a little girl's. "I'm going in tomorrow morning. I haven't been answering my phone in case they wanted to come over here and question me. I'm not stupid. I know Brent doesn't care for me much. But I l...l...love him and don't want to h...h...hurt him," she stuttered.

This was too painful for words. I couldn't say anything in reply. I walked over to her and put my hand on her shoulder. She might be young and naïve, but fraud is fraud. It was obvious from her distress she knew exactly what Brent was in for. They weren't just going to slap his wrists and hand him back his saucepan.

"Do you think he'll get in a lot of trouble?" she whimpered.

I didn't want to lie anymore so I said nothing.

She turned her back to me, lay down on the bed, and pulled her covers over her head. "Could you go now?" came a muffled voice from the other side of the bed.

I knew from her voice she'd let loose and bawl like a banshee when I finally made my exit. The Italian ceramics and Venetian goblets weren't going to keep him forever. It was just a matter of time before her very simplicity and vulnerability became boring and irritating. This murder ended it much sooner than she'd anticipated.

I let myself out. I looked at my watch. Nine o'clock. I needed food right away and a twenty-four-hour Safeway was pretty close by. Bruschetta piled high with tomatoes would hit the spot right about now.

When I got home my answering machine was blinking like mad. The first ten messages were mainly from friends chastising me for not calling them back. Those I ignored. My mother left three messages, each sounding more worried than the one before. Even though it was after ten o'clock, I phoned her right back. I knew she'd be sitting at the kitchen table waiting for me to call and driving my stepfather crazy by asking him every three minutes, "Where do you think she is? Why hasn't she called back?" I got off the phone in record time by pleading extreme exhaustion. Message eleven was from Jim.

"Mary, I want to talk to you for five minutes," he pleaded. "Don't...Look, please call me." I'd leave a message on his machine in the morning when he was at work. I didn't need him *and* my mother calling me every ten minutes to check on my whereabouts.

The next message was from a Latino male voice I couldn't place. "*Señora* Ryan?" He paused for five seconds, then hung up. His voice sounded familiar, but there was too much background noise for me to tell who it was. Gilberto maybe?

Message thirteen was from my sister, Nora.

"Mary, just calling to hope you're okay. I'll try calling back later."

Her kids were screaming in the background; fun screaming, not killing each other screaming. We hadn't spoken much in the last few months. Naturally her conversations would be filled with how Laura was doing in school, Kevin's grades, will Timmy have to get braces or not, did Dan get that big promotion. My end of the conversation was limited to the numbers of hours I'd worked that week and the grief I was getting from my therapist about not letting go of my failed marriage.

Since my divorce, my loneliness and despair over not having any children magnified tenfold every time I spoke to her. I stopped calling her, and sent her funny cards with risqué sayings on them in lieu of real conversation. It just hurt too much to talk to her. I hoped she understood. Time to mail another card telling her I was fine.

Message fourteen was from Juan, overflowing with mea culpas. "Mary, I am so sorry for my behavior today. You must think I have no manners. I was so distressed over the events of the last two days, I took out my frustrations on that poor deliveryman. You can rest assured it will not happen again. Please accept my most fervent apologies."

He went on in this vein for a while so I tuned out. I can only handle so much of Juan's excessive courtesy. In my meaner moments I call him the Latin Uriah Heep. It goes over very well with the socialites he has to deal with on a daily basis. These people thrive on obsequious behavior, but I find it suffocating.

Then the tone of his voice changed and caught my interest again. "And the funeral for Carlos is Tuesday morning, ten o'clock, at St. Boniface in the Mission. There will be a reception in the church hall following the service. I phoned the staff to let them know. Please call me back if you have any questions. And again, I apologize for my boorish behavior today."

Guilt reigned. Two minutes earlier I'd been mentally trashing this guy, now I find out he's gone to the trouble to call all the staff and let them know about Carlos' funeral. I must be nice to him at the church and let him know how much I appreciated his efforts.

The rest of the messages were from other chefs begging me to call them back and let them know what the scoop on the murder was. I cleared my answering machine. I went into my dining room and poured myself a large cognac. Sitting in my dark living room, I held my own little private wake for Carlos.

Carlos would bring me exotic fruits from markets in the Mission, prefacing his gifts with, "These aren't as good as the kind we have in El Salvador, but..." and then shrug his shoulders. How was his family going to make it without him? Like most of the Latinos I worked with, he worked two jobs— to support his family here and to send money back to his relatives in El Salvador.

I fell asleep on the couch and woke up around eight, my neck aching as if I'd been wearing a watermelon as a necklace all night. After fortifying myself with a couple of Motrin and a hot shower, I got dressed.

I had a whole day ahead of me: what to do?

The more entrenched you become in the food business, the more it consumes your whole life until your only friends are foodies, your leisure activities center on food; your idea of a good time is to eat at the latest restaurant. There's a great line in the movie *Moonstruck* when Nicholas Cage, who is a baker, yells, "I have no life." Nobody but food people gets that line; they're rolling in the aisles. But it's that kind of laughter with a heavy dose of hysteria attached to it.

Vowing to do something non-food related, I picked up the paint chips piled in a heap on my dining room table. Trying to visualize different colors in various rooms forced me to look at the house for the first time in months. What a pigsty.

O'Connor called as I was scrubbing the grout in my bathroom with an old toothbrush and bleach.

"Hey, Ryan, you holding up?"

"What do you want, O'Connor?" I cupped the portable phone in my ear and went back to the grout.

"Are you going to the funeral on Tuesday?"

"Of course I'm going to the funeral."

"Look, I'll be there, too. Keep your eyeballs peeled for his brother and point him out to me if he shows."

I stopped cleaning the grout, the toothbrush suspended in midair. "Don't tell me you suspect his brother? I've worked with these guys for five years. Gilberto wouldn't hurt a fly, much less his brother."

"Get rid of that attitude, Ryan. I've talked to everybody who works at the restaurant. Nobody's seen this guy. Don't you think it's strange he's disappeared?"

Gilberto hadn't exactly disappeared. I didn't say anything about the phone call I had gotten or spotting him at the paint store. I needed to see Gilberto and talk to him.

"Anyway, I'll save you a seat. I'll be in a pew in the very back row. By the way, how long has it been since you've been in a church, Mary?"

"I can do without your snide remarks, O'Connor," I snarled into the phone, but he had already hung up.

I kept on cleaning, moving methodically from room to room. In the middle of this cleaning frenzy I realized I was beginning to feel like me again. Pre-divorce Mary. It took a murder to shake me out of this awful combination of constant lethargy and simmering anger that had imprisoned me since my divorce. I was finally paying attention to someone other than me. Carlos' murder was the slap on both cheeks. My anger was the ultimate exercise in narcissism. Only my loneliness mattered, only my anger was justified. My voice was always on the verge of a scream. Christ, I was tired of yelling.

For the first time in two years I felt alive, awake, not so much as a trace of bitterness in my swallow. I actually looked at things. The floors needed refinishing; the light fixtures were unbelievably ugly. I had no pictures on my walls, the piano needed tuning.

But the best part was that I was hungry, with a glorious healthy hunger, not the kind where you fill a hole to keep on moving. I wanted a full-blown meal, not junk food. I wanted some sort of gooey pasta, a Grace Baking Stormy sourdough baguette for mopping up the sauce, and light Chianti to chase it with. I craved a simple salad of mixed greens with a tart vinegary balsamic dressing. For dessert I envisioned a slice of Gorgonzola from Peck's, a perfectly ripe pear, and an espresso laced with cognac. I practically had an orgasm on the spot thinking about it.

Before my divorce, I truly loved food. Not only did I love eating it, I loved making it. No matter how frustrated I'd been with my various jobs, I'd never lost that pure joy of mixing butter and sugar to just the right consistency so that the eggs incorporated smoothly and the batter wouldn't break. Or the pleasant monotony of rolling croissants. Or the sensuous smell of chocolate wafting over you as you melt it, infusing your chef's jacket and hair with a heavy sexy aroma so that when you brush your hair before you go to bed at night your bathroom smells like chocolate. After Jim left, all of it vanished.

Now when I smell chocolate in my hair after a long day I want to throwup. The more I cleaned the more I realized self-revelations weren't going to come if I was working sixty-five hours a week. I'd tell Brent next week I was quitting. I had six months' worth of living expenses in the bank. I should be able to get my act together by then.

I felt so empowered by these thoughts that I actually called Jim and left a semi-polite message. "Jim, it's Mary. I feel perfectly safe. Don't worry about me. Don't call me again." Click. Well, I tried to be polite.

It was six o'clock by the time I finished cleaning my house. In honor of my industry, I decided to treat myself to a nice place for dinner. I had my car key in the lock when O'Connor pulled up. He got out of the car, his arms filled with grocery bags.

"You're not going anywhere, Ryan," O'Connor ordered. "Get that skinny ass back inside and help me make dinner."

We met at the path to my front door. I grinned and pointed at the grocery bags. "I hope there's food in there. I'm ravenous."

When we got inside, he dumped the groceries on my kitchen table and looked me over. "I figured you didn't have any food in the house. Did you have lunch today?"

"Yes, I did," I said hotly. No need to tell him it was a box of Altoids.

He looked me over and shook his head. "Skinny is not a look you should cultivate."

I stuck my tongue out at him.

My stomach grumbled in grateful anticipation as we unloaded the groceries: nestled strands of fresh linguine, paper-thin slices of pancetta, a wedge of parmesan, a big bag of mixed spring greens, a container of sungold tomatoes, a bottle of Chianti, and two large truffles for dessert.

The greatest thing about the food evolution of the nineteen eighties was not that we got to throw our money away on overpriced restaurant food, but that it educated people and forced the supermarkets to upscale their assortment to remain competitive and attract those customers who crave something a little more appetizing than pork and beans from a can.

"I make the pasta, you do the salad and set the table?" O'Connor brokered.

"Deal."

First, I got out two Waterford crystal goblets and poured both of us a generous helping of wine. Next, I set the table with my finest china and crystal. I hadn't had a decent meal in a long time. I mean decent in the sense of a complete dining experience where it's not only the food that's important, but the entire package: the crystal magnifies the luster of a wine, the china frames the food like a fine painting, and the candlelight softens everything in its gentle glow.

The aroma of sautéed pancetta competed with the pungent odor of the balsamic vinegar as I whisked together a tart dressing.

"O'Connor, heads up." I popped a couple of tomatoes in my mouth, then I tossed a tomato his way and he scooped it up with his jaw. We smiled at each other as the sweet juice filled our cheeks.

By eight o'clock we were thoroughly sated and drinking espressos thick enough to clog pipes. You can tell where my priorities are. All of my windowsills need repainting, but I've the latest and greatest espresso machine.

While savoring my coffee, I began conducting this internal debate whether or not to tell O'Connor about my little adventures with Brent and Gilberto. The episode with the files in the office was bizarre.

O'Connor coughed discreetly and broke into my reverie. I realized that I'd been staring into space with my head going right or left depending on which side of the argument I was on.

"Your neck bothering you, Ryan?"

I blushed. "Yeah, my neck is a little stiff. I fell asleep on the couch last night."

Maybe I'll just casually broach the subject of the murder, I thought, see if anything weird had come up, and then segue into my own information.

"So, how's the investigation going?"

"We talked to the wife today."

I stifled an urge to kick him under the table and managed to say quietly, "Her name's Rosa."

O'Connor ignored me. "He had three kids under the age of four and there's another one on the way. You wonder how they're going to make it," he said, echoing my own concerns of last night. "Don't these people know about birth control?"

The sleepy camaraderie of the last hour shattered. I slammed down my espresso cup. "I'd like to point out that these people, as you so rudely refer to them, are not the only couple I know who have three kids under the age of four," reminding him of his own progeny.

"My children were planned and wanted," he snapped back at me.

"What makes you think these children weren't planned and aren't wanted? Did his children look malnourished or underfed? Carlos might not have made the big bucks detectives do, but he worked like an absolute dog to support his family."

"Oh, Christ," he groaned. He stood up, came over to my chair, bent down, and grabbed me by the shoulders. We locked eyes, our collective anger heating the room up by five degrees. "Can't we sit here and have a nice meal without you turning it into some sort of political referendum? What is it with you?"

We stared at each other for ten seconds, then he abruptly let go of me as if my shoulders made his hands burn and stomped out the front door.

I can't go to bed with dirty dishes in the sink, so I washed up, ranting and raving to myself about the stupidity of cops. I was putting away the wineglasses when the phone rang. O'Connor calling to apologize, I thought.

I wove the stems of the wineglasses between my fingers and picked up the phone with my free hand. "Hello," I said, trying not to smirk.

"Mind your own business. Cunt!" a voice screamed into my ear.

Chapter 9

The wineglasses slipped out of my limp fingers and shattered on the hardwood floor.

I swept up one hundred and sixty dollars worth of Waterford crystal shards and thought about the phone call. There was a lot of background noise, as if the caller were standing in a telephone booth on a busy street like Van Ness. I couldn't detect any sort of accent, nor was the voice particularly high or low. Should I call O'Connor? Unbidden, Jim's name popped up. Should I call him?

None of the above. My mother? No way. If I told her about the phone call, she'd chain me to her kitchen table. Jim was out for obvious reasons. O'Connor? "No, I can't identify the voice. No, it was too noisy for me to make out anything." I'd sound like a moron. And the truth be told, I was still pissed off at him. Sexist, fascist, racist jerk.

Then it came to me. Brent. He was still ticked off that I'd talked with Teri. I had a hard time imagining him using that word, but then again I wouldn't have pegged him for tax fraud either. I didn't need to call O'Connor. I could handle Brent.

Getting ready for bed, I remembered a message left on my machine by someone who might have a little more insight into the financial end of things. Camille Chinamino.

Camille and I'd gone to École d'Epicure together. Close friends in school, our relationship had dwindled down to having dinner together once or twice a year. While I went the more traditional post-graduation route by working in restaurants, she became a food writer. Currently she's writing the weekly food gossip column for the *San Francisco Chronicle.* You know, what chef is cooking where, which restaurants are opening and closing, and, most important, who's financially backing whom. Her column is as closely read as the financial writers. San Francisco is a food town, a mecca for people who like to eat. Patrons follow their favorite chefs from venue to venue, commiserate over hard-to-come-by reservations, and diss menus. There are only really three food towns in the U.S.: New York, New Orleans, and San Francisco. By that I mean places where you'd plan a vacation and buy airline tickets solely based on the restaurant scene. Chicago is creeping in there, but only because of Charlie Trotter's. Ditto for Boston and Todd English.

Before I called her back, I mapped out a plan so I'd get the answers I needed, but not make her unduly curious. I was in luck, she was home.

"Camille, it's Mary."

"Mary, I've called and called. Where have you been? I've called you about fifty…Jasper, I've told you for the last time, your food is over there." I heard plaintive meowing in the background. Camille adopts stray cats and then pesters her friends to give them permanent homes. Inevitably, she'll turn into one of those old women who leave their estates to the SPCA. "Cleo, stop that. What's the latest? My deadline is tomorrow morning, and my editor would be the cat that ate the canary if I had something original."

An interesting choice of words considering she was knee-deep in cats.

"Sorry to disappoint you, Camille. I really don't have any more information than what your own paper printed." Despite gorging myself at dinner, I was starving. I perched the phone on one ear and started slicing into what was left of the baguette. "It was one of my pastry guys, but the cops still don't have a motive."

"Mary, are you there? This phone connection is terrible. I can't hear you. It sounds like someone's sawing wood."

"Uh, let me punch some buttons." I sliced through the rest of the baguette and put down the knife. "Is that better?"

"Yeah, these portable phones. Can't live with 'em, can't live without 'em. Here's your dinner, Mouser." Camille's love affair with animals was a constant reminder to me about the pitfalls of being single. When cats become your only bed partner, it's time to start running singles ads in every paper within two hundred miles. "Call up Jim. What are ex-husbands who happen to be a homicide inspectors for?"

"Camille," I admonished, "you know that Jim and I aren't exactly on speaking terms. Besides, I can't tell you anything about the murder itself. The detective in charge would cut off my ears and sauté them for his breakfast if I told you the crime scene details. I called because I've a big favor to ask of you."

I lathered the bread with a two-inch slab of sweet butter. "This probably isn't very newsworthy, but do you think you could put a paragraph in about what a nice guy Carlos was, how he's going to be missed, and so on. He had a great sense of humor and was always smiling, despite the fact he worked two jobs."

"Sure, no problem. I can squeeze it in below Wolfgang's newest place opening in Vegas."

"There's more. This is the biggee, Camille. Could you set up some sort of fund through the paper to help his family? He's got…had three kids and his wife's pregnant." I had to stop for a couple of seconds to pull myself together. "I'd really appreciate it."

"No problem, kiddo. I think I can bump the paragraph I was writing about the mayor getting pied in the face again. I can tell from your voice, you really liked him, didn't you?"

"Yeah, I did. He worked his ass off for me. If I had asked him to plunge his right arm into a deep fat fryer he would have."

I needed to change this train of thought or I'd be guzzling the cognac again.

"Camille, while I have you on the line. I've a question about backers. I'm toying with the idea of opening my own bakery. I read your column last week about Norm and Polly opening up their new place. How did they get the money? They had Lars design the restaurant, for chrissakes, and he doesn't come cheap. And the last time I checked, those Italian hand-built bread ovens are pretty pricey." I took a big bite of bread. Ummm, heaven on earth.

"Well, Polly has family money and Norm charmed some Silicon Valley millionaires. I talked to them a couple of months ago. They told me construction costs had ballooned to four million by the end. Fortunately, they got a good review last week. Otherwise I bet they'd be sharpening their knives right about now to cut their throats. The light fixtures Karlsen designed for the dining room were a thousand apiece."

Opening a restaurant is big business these days. Nobody rounds up used bentwood chairs and covers tables with red-checked tablecloths anymore. If you hire a restaurant designer chances are you'll sink anywhere from one to two million bucks into the place even before you open the door. Of course, the irony is that eighty percent of all restaurants fail within two years of opening. The restaurant business is the toughest game in town.

"When Brent opened American Fare, I completely ignored that part of it. I should get more involved in the financial end of things. Do you know who financed him? I'll see him at the funeral, but since I have you on the phone…" I took another big bite.

"Beats me. He said something vague about profits from some investments. Who's his broker, Hillary Clinton? Every time I brought it up, he changed the subject. Did you guys use Lars? I can't remember."

"No, Brent didn't want anything too stylized. He went to France and visited about a hundred different bistros trying to come up with a timeless look."

"You guys swamped?"

I thought about the hours of overtime I'd be putting in over the next couple of months. The cords in my neck started to clump in tight knots.

"Of course, with more fresh hell in store. I don't know how long I can muster up the energy to do this."

"That's why I went into food writing. With my bad back I figured a career actually cooking was short-lived. It amazes me that Brent has the energy to have all those affairs. Is he still fooling around with that rich blonde?"

I haven't seen any statistics, but I bet the divorce rate for chefs is up there with doctors and lawyers. The food business attracts young people because they'll work for the low wages restaurants typically pay, and they have the superhuman energy needed in a kitchen. This means middle-aged chefs hit on a lot of twenty-year-old women. I don't know if older women chefs are hitting on young virile waiters; it could be now that there are more women in the profession, but I doubt it. As a woman chef you have to work even harder to prove yourself. I doubt whether any of my fellow female chefs have the energy.

"Yeah, among others."

"Are you seeing anyone? Oh, just a minute." The phone made a sharp thunk. I could hear her faintly, as if she was in another room: "Don't shred Mommy's new Coach handbag, Mittens. It's vewwwy expensive," she admonished in an Elmer Fudd voice.

I'd better make that dinner reservation fast. Camille needed to get out more. As far as I was concerned, speaking to cats in cartoon voices is one step away from believing *National Enquirer* headlines.

"Sorry about that," Camille apologized. "Cats, you've got to love them. So, are you dating yet? And don't give me that line about how you're not ready. It's been almost two years."

"These days I barely have the energy to brush my teeth, Camille. I just can't be nice to anyone right now. I'm seriously thinking of quitting and taking some time off. Of course, I'll let you know when I give notice so you can put it in your column. This murder has made me stop banging my head against the wall. I want to rebuild my life. I owe you dinner. At Masa's no less."

"It's creepy isn't it? That they never found out who murdered him."

Masa Kobayashi was *the* chef in San Francisco, if not the entire United States, during the nineteen eighties. One of the top chefs in the world, no contest. Until he was found murdered, beaten to death, in the corridor of his apartment building. An unassuming man with an almost ungodly ability with food, he had no known enemies. The rumor around the cooking community was that he got behind in some gambling debts. Moral of the story, do not mess with the Chinese gangs in San Francisco.

"Yeah, it had me looking over my shoulder for a few days. Hey, thanks so much for the plug about Carlos."

"No sweat. My editor loves human-interest stuff every now and then. Keeps the column from being just a series of advertisements plugging new restaurants. I'll let you know about how the fund is doing in a couple of weeks."

"Sounds great. We'll set up our dinner date then. And before you ask, I'm not taking any cats."

"Seriously, Mary, it might help with the loneliness. I've got two wonderful little kittens…"

"Maybe later. Bye."

While wolfing down the rest of the baguette, I mulled over our conversation. Instead of getting answers, I was stuck with more questions.

What I told Camille was true. I hadn't thought about all the money it must have taken to put American Fare on the map. We hadn't hired Lars, but Brent had still spent a fortune on the dining room and a fortune-plus on the kitchen. Every appliance, every ladle was top of the line. He gave me carte blanche to order any equipment I wanted. At the time I was like a kid in a candy store, picking out heart-shaped pie pans,

Spode china to showcase my desserts, Swiss chocolate molds, whatever caught my fancy.

But where had the money come from?

Brent doesn't talk about his childhood much, but from the little he's said, I gained the impression his family was pretty poor. Brent's father worked the oil rigs throughout Colorado and Texas. The work wasn't steady, and it sounded like Dad had a major problem with the sauce. Brent had worked in greasy spoons the minute he was tall enough to push a broom, earning money to help feed the family. I doubt "family money" would apply in this case.

Dismissing that ludicrous story about investments, who actually owned American Fare?

I spent all day Sunday working on my yard. Although gardening is one of my passions, I hadn't so much as turned over a single dirt clod the entire year I had lived in this house. Somehow the grass was surviving my total neglect.

While ripping out a bunch of tired geraniums, I searched my memory for any conversations Brent and I'd had about opening up American Fare and the financial setup. I couldn't come up with a single one, which is not to say they didn't happen. We probably talked about it at length, but I'd tuned it out. I find money boring; I barely bother to reconcile my own checkbook. He might keep that information from Camille. She'd have blabbed about his business affairs to every chef from here to New York. But why keep it a secret from me? I might not remember the money part, but a partner I'd remember.

Where could I find out about the financial setup? I couldn't exactly ask Brent; clearly he thought I was already a little too involved in his affairs as it was. It hit me. Right after Camille and I graduated from school, we started a weekend catering business and had to get a business license at the Office of

Consumer Affairs. I'd go to City Hall and search their files. All that stuff should be public record.

After working hard in the garden all day, I slept like the dead and was up at dawn. I made myself a latte to go and hit the doughnut shop on my way out of town. I was at City Hall at nine. No sign of a blue van in the rearview mirror.

The room where the business license records were housed was painted that government issue, pukey, pastel green. A long Formica counter bisected the room, and a maze of cubicles sat behind the counter. No sounds of life, not even the click of computer keys. I pushed down on a bell ringer like the crudely hand-lettered sign indicated. I was on my best behavior today.

I counted to ten. No one appeared. I pushed the bell again. Twice.

A head peeped around the corner of a cubicle wall. A woman in her late forties with a home frost job and bad Farrah Fawcett haircut glared at me. Her face had that gray-white pallor of someone who smoked two packs a day and considered potato chips a vegetable.

"Hi," I smiled. "I need to get some information about business licenses?"

"Fill out forms 601b and 603c. Ring when you're done," she ordered in a gravelly monotone, and her head immediately whipped back behind the cubicle. The computer voice that gives out phone numbers when you dial 411 had more personality.

"Excuse me," I said in a loud but polite voice. She couldn't have walked out of earshot. The room wasn't *that* big. "I don't want a business license, I want to look up some public records."

No head.

"Excuse me?" I said louder, still in polite mode, although I felt a big ass frown pulling at the sides of my mouth. I counted to ten again.

Still no head.

Sigh. These days polite doesn't get you anywhere. Time for evil Mary to make an appearance. I began singing and dinging "It's a Small World" on the bell. It's toss-up what's more annoying, the song or my voice, which has been likened to the sound chickens make as they're being killed.

I got through only two lines before she reappeared, stomping out from the labyrinth of cubicles, her pallor thrown into stark relief by the twin spots of rage on both cheeks.

"Sorry to disturb your solitaire game," I apologized. "But I don't need to fill out any forms. I want to look up a business license."

She raised her arm in a stiff, Ghost of Christmas Future manner, and pointed in the direction of a computer at the far end of the room. Then she scooped up the ringer, narrowed her eyes in a glare that would crack an egg, and stomped back to her desk.

"Thank you so much for all your help," I yelled to her back.

For all my recent bitching about the cooking world, I found myself silently counting my blessings. Instead of caramelizing apples over the stovetop for tarte tartin, the aroma of the burnt sugar tickling my nose, it could be me working in a four-foot by six-foot cubicle, repeating the same instructions over and over again to snotty women with attitude. The highlight of my week would be to win twenty games of solitaire as opposed to the nineteen I won last week.

Fortunately, the computer was designed for techie-challenged individuals like myself. I was so pumped up I could barely keep my butt in the seat while waiting for the information to come up on the screen.

The computer groaned and complained at the typed requests, and finally coughed up what I needed. I searched through all the little boxes of information and finally found the box listing the owner.

Goddamn it, Brent was indeed an owner, but there was a second owner: Vino Blanco Corporation.

Over the years, Brent had inundated me with his plans for the restaurant he would one day own: what it would look like, the menu, even the type of cutlery he wanted. But never in all this pie-in-the-sky talk had he once mentioned Vino Blanco. Who could forget White Wine Corporation? It sounded like a think tank for Tenderloin winos. Fortunately, there was an address on Mission Street, somewhere around 17th Street judging by the number.

Time to check out Vino Blanco in person.

City Hall isn't far from the Mission and luckily I found a parking space just off 17th.

I love the Mission. It's the only place left in San Francisco with street life. North Beach has sacrificed almost all its ethnicity in pursuit of chic. The death knell began tolling when the U.S. Restaurant closed its doors and will finish when Molinari's goes dark. There are still a few cafes where you can hear Italians arguing with each other, but by and large it's a lot of people dressed in black talking on cell phones. And while Chinatown can't be beat for its produce, everyone is in a rush. They have to get home or go the store or catch the Stockton bus. Mothers silently hustle their children down the street. The only sounds you hear are chickens squawking and shoppers haggling with storekeepers.

In the Mission, people saunter, they loiter. Men check out the chicas, the chicas flirt with the men and reapply their lipliner every fifteen minutes. The smell of cooked goat wafts out of the doors of funky taquerias, the sort of places that you know are going to give you the runs the next day, but you eat there anyway because it smells so good. Rap pours out of car windows and from random boom boxes. Fruit and vegetables pyramided in makeshift produce stands line the sidewalks. Kids squeal and laugh at their own antics as their mothers gracefully weave them in and out of the crowds. You can walk seven blocks and never hear a word of English.

The Mission was two coffin nails from extinction during the dot-com frenzy of the nineteen nineties. Computer start-ups spilled out of South Park hungry for rental space. Car mechanics, small manufacturers, sheet metal shops, and cheap outlet stores found their rents tripling and quadrupling when their leases were up. The implosion of the dot-com phenomenon has temporarily halted the Mission's demise. When a Starbucks appears I'll know the Mission will be virtually dead, gentrification only a frappucino away.

I stopped in front of the address I'd written down on my wrist. I checked it again. In front of me was a particularly divey taqueria. I could see three tables and four chairs through the open door, all mismatched. The windows didn't look like they'd been washed since the Kennedy Administration, and the awning leaning over the windows was tattered. It didn't even have a name.

The taqueria was empty. I walked in. Two older Latino men stood behind the counter, one desultorily chopping up grilled flank steak and the other dicing tomatoes. They both had that hunched-shoulder look from a near lifetime of keeping their heads bowed and their mouths shut.

Neither man looked up when I approached the counter.

This was going to be tough. Not for the first time did I curse myself for not taking some basic Spanish classes. My Spanish was *very* limited.

"*Hola,*" I said in a chirpy, isn't-it-a-lovely-day voice. "*Por favor, Señor?*" No reaction; both of them went on chopping. They didn't raise their heads one inch.

"Excuse me," I said louder. Still no reaction. Did I have my invisibility cloak on today? Why weren't people answering my questions?

A small, heavyset man with deep-set black eyes and tufts of hair growing from his ears appeared from the back of the restaurant. He stood very close to the cash register, like I was going to rob the place. He wore a faded red tee shirt, with large perspiration rings under the arms.

"*Señor,*" I began. "*Donde esta Vino Blanco Corporation? Habla Ingles?*" And that was the extent of my Spanish. I hoped the man spoke more English than I spoke Spanish.

The chopping stopped. I looked over toward where the other men were working. They stared at me, their knives suspended in the air.

Never taking his eyes off me, the man guarding the cash register said something in rapid-fire Spanish out of the corner of his mouth. Both workers dropped their knives and ran through the door leading to the back.

"*No comprende*," the heavyset man snapped at me.

Concentrating on the two men sprinting out the back door, I missed the first part of what he said. He moved over to the chopping block, grabbed the cleaver, and poised it over the cutting board.

"Excuse me," I repeated.

"*No*"—thwack went the cleaver. Meat went flying in all directions from the force of the knife. "*Comprende*"—thwack again. "*Señora*"—thwack, he repeated in a loud, slow voice, as if I was hard of hearing.

"Vino Blanco Corporation, *aquí*?" I pointed to the floor.

Instantly, his eyes darkened and the cords on his neck began to bulge. It was like watching a bull warming up to gore someone to death. He raised the cleaver shoulder height, threw back his arm, and aimed the cleaver right at my forehead.

I ran.

Chapter 10

Car, car, get to the car, I told myself over and over. I'm naturally clumsy, but that morning God granted me a stay of execution from my big feet. Like a ballerina on fast forward, I pranced and hopped in between and around people in a frantic effort to reach my car before some beefy paw grabbed my shoulder. Once safely inside the car with all the doors locked, I hugged my steering wheel in relief.

As I put the key in the ignition an image of that thug in the taqueria, his fat hands around my neck, did make me consider going home and forgetting this whole thing, but only for a millisecond. I was management. Not a few eyebrows would skyrocket if American Fare tanked because of questionable business practices. I'd spend the next three years looking for work, trying to convince people that I was clueless to Brent's shenanigans. Or worse, pleading with some D.A. that I was innocent of any wrongdoing.

I drove down Mission to the Fifth Street garage, parked in a well-populated section of the garage, and planned my next move. I wouldn't do anything stupid. I'd stay away from the Mission and do my sleuthing some place safe. Like the Financial District.

How do you set up a corporation?

I mentally kicked myself for cutting all those business classes while at cooking school. If I had attended a few, maybe I wouldn't have to drive down to the Embarcadero and face

Dominique Porcella: corporate attorney, friend to the mayor, confidant to big business—and my uncle.

Uncle Dom is a partner at a 101 California law firm that has earned a permanent home in Dante's fourth circle of hell. Apolitical in a town infamous for its politics, their primary function is to make the rich richer. House lawyers for many of the big developers, Winston, White, Howe, and Porcella's fingers are in most of the financial pies in town.

A receptionist with a phone cradled on her shoulder scoped me out the four seconds it took me to walk from the elevator to her desk. My faded black tee shirt, down vest, and wrinkled khakis didn't pass muster. Probably thinking I was part of the janitorial crew, she ignored me and continued to chat on the phone. I could tell it was a personal call. She kept twirling her hair with an index finger and giggling in a breathy, heavy tone that suggested one-way phone sex. The black suit, lips outlined in that fashionable dark liner/light mauvy infill with nail color to match, and a profusion of blonde, Ophelia-like hair made her look like a vampire in training.

I waved a polite little hello close enough to her face to get her attention, but not close enough to be rude, and mouthed an "Excuse me." She swiveled a couple of inches away from me and giggled some more.

"Excuse me," I said aloud.

She swiveled her chair completely away from me so that I faced her back. The final straw was when she flicked her wrist at me, in a pert, cool-your-jets sort of motion.

That was the third time today. I was sick of people ignoring me.

I marched around the curve of the desk to where she was sitting and yanked the phone out of her hand.

"I'm sorry, the person you are phone fucking has to return to work now. If you continue to call her at work, she will be fired. Good-bye." I slammed the phone down.

"Hey, what do you think you're doing," she screeched. "If you don't move your ass on the elevator right now, I'm going to call security." She shook her mass of blond, moussed ringlets in the direction of the elevator and picked up the phone to make good her threat.

Am I the only person in the continental United States who doesn't own a canister of mousse?

"Hey," I snapped back. "I happen to be Dominique Porcella's niece. I would greatly appreciate it if you would ring him immediately and tell him that Ms. Ryan is here for her appointment."

I didn't have an appointment, but she didn't have to know that.

The mention of Uncle Dom's name and the rage vanished from her face. As if he were in the room scowling in disapproval, her hands swung the hair back off her face, she checked her collar to make sure it hadn't crept under the jacket, and tugged on the jacket to make sure it was smooth.

Without making eye contact she said, "I'm sorry Ms. Ryan, I'll ring Mr. Porcella's private secretary right away." She grabbed the phone and punched the button with the end of a pencil because her nails were so long. "Ruthie, Ms. Ryan is here for her 11:30 with Mr. Porcella."

I crossed my fingers. Be there, I prayed.

"You may go in now, Ms. Ryan," she mumbled to her desk blotter and buzzed the security door for me to go through.

"Thank you very much," I said to the top of her head.

I normally don't pull that kind of power play, but in the Financial District if you're not dressed for the part, you're invisible. No Donna Karan suit, no eye contact. No Rolex, no courtesy. It pisses me off.

I walked down miles of corridor to a coveted corner office and knocked.

"Come in," a deep voice ordered.

As usual, Uncle Dom was on the phone, reading a brief, and typing on a computer. His attention is never focused on one thing, two at a minimum, four for him to be perfectly happy.

I've often thought he's a manic-depressive, but conveniently missing the depressive part.

"Walter, I've got a lunch date with Willie in fifteen minutes. I'll update you when I return. I don't anticipate any problems."

Uncle Dom never does. My condolences to the people who attempt to cause him problems.

The headset came off, the laptop was snapped shut, the brief was returned to its folder and placed precisely in the middle of his desk. Having gone completely gray by forty, he hasn't aged one iota in twenty-five years. Enemies and relatives call him "Domian Grey" behind his back. He has those strong Italian features that made him gawky at twenty but handsome at forty. A face that gradually came into its own and stayed there.

He stood up and walked across the room with the energy of a twenty-year-old and flicked a quick eye over my attire; he didn't bother to hide his disgust. His suits were made in Hong Kong, his shirts in London. In a previous visit to his office he had handed me a check for $3000 and ordered me to buy some decent clothes. I'm embarrassed to admit I accepted it, then ran down the street to Williams Sonoma and bought enough copper pots to rival the kitchen at Buckingham Palace.

"Mary, we can talk while I walk to Jack's. I've a lunch date with the mayor," and he was out the door, me trailing in his wake.

Not a word passed between us until we were out on the street. At a clip I would describe as a trot, we strode up California Street. If Uncle Dom did this every day, no wonder he was in such great shape. He had thirty years on me and I was gasping for breath and sweating from pores I'd no idea I possessed. He didn't even look like he was breathing.

"I accept your apology, Mary."

We'd gotten into a fight during Christmas dinner over the recent escalating number of pedophile cases involving priests and altar boys and hadn't spoken to each other since.

A devout Catholic who attends Mass every day, he dismissed it as a bunch of troubled youths at the mercy of unscrupulous psychologists and incompetent lawyers. I countered that every gay man I knew who'd been an altar boy had had his first sexual experience with a priest. A bad move on my part. His eldest son, my cousin Joe, was a priest.

"I'm not here to apologize, Uncle Dom," I panted. "I was *not* implying that Joe is a pedophile. And if we were adding up insults, I never received an apology for that rude comment you made about me wasting my brains and going blue collar just to spite my family."

It had been an ugly fight. It began with him accusing me of saying anything to slander the church, even to the point of calling his son a child molester, and ended with him telling me I was a disgrace to the family and that I should get a real job. His antagonism toward my profession was all the stranger as his own parents had owned a mom-and-pop bakery in North Beach for years. I don't know what offended him more, my atheism or going into "trade" as he called it.

I put my hand on his arm.

"Look, I need some information about setting up corporations. If you don't want to help me, I'll go *outside* the family," I emphasized.

His pace slowed just a fraction, and I knew he was weighing the potential consequences of Dom Porcella's niece asking other attorneys for advice. If that got around town…he patted my hand in a manner implying forgiveness and benediction.

We turned onto Montgomery and a relatively flat landscape. Maybe I'd survive this walk without going into heart failure.

Jack's is beautiful. Arguably the oldest restaurant in San Francisco, the gold filigree ceilings, wall-to-wall mirrors, thick bunches of cream-colored roses spilling out of crystal vases all give it a Golden Age charm. Whenever I eat there I'm always a little shocked to see diners in modern dress. It's the sort of restaurant where you would expect to see characters from an Edith Wharton novel at the table next to yours.

"Hello, Mr. Porcella." The maître d' beamed a big, can't-wait-to-get-my-cut-of-the-gratuity smile at my uncle. His fussy, over-trimmed mustache, bow tie, and shaved head reminded me of an egg in disguise. "Mr. Mayor is running a little late."

He ignored me completely. A fly on the shoulder of Uncle Dom's jacket would've gotten more attention. San Francisco is still a man's domain. Except for a select few, women are relegated to being the wife, the mistress, or the secretary.

"As always, eh, Howard," my uncle chuckled.

The two of them probably repeated this conversation at least once a week.

"Howard, this is my niece, Mary Ryan."

Uncle Dom might be a corporate shark willing to sell his own mother for stock options, but he is polite in the old world, treat your womenfolk well, sort of way. Not five seconds earlier, I didn't rate a soupçon of acknowledgment, now I got my own beam of approval.

"Very pleased to meet you, Ms. Ryan," Howard gushed and smirked. I returned an equally insincere smirk. "Will you be joining Mr. Porcella and the Mayor for lunch?"

It is not often that I see my uncle nonplussed. A look of horror crossed his face at the thought of his ragtag niece spoiling his power lunch with the mayor.

"No, I have another engagement." I smiled sweetly. "Uncle Dom, why don't we have a quick glass of champagne while you wait for the mayor?"

Now that we had made peace, we chitchatted about my aunt and cousins until the champagne arrived. Forty years ago my Aunt Mary shocked her Irish relatives by marrying this awkward Italian kid just out of law school. No one could have predicted that the two of them would "out-Catholic" us all, having eight children and graduating to a first-name basis with every cardinal in the United States.

The waiter filled our flutes with Veuve Clicquot. I took a tiny sip; it was as fresh and light as a first kiss. In the middle of savoring the second, much larger sip, Uncle Dom's voice brought me back to the present.

"What do you need to know, Mary?"

I blinked at him, confused. I was so engrossed in the champagne that I had completely forgotten why I was here.

"Uh, right." I hadn't given any thought to how to handle this. I didn't want to give Uncle Dom the impression that American Fare was doing anything illegal. "I'm thinking of opening my own restaurant. I'm assuming that I need to be incorporated and, of course, I thought you'd be able to give me the best advice."

"The tax breaks are enormous, well worth your effort." Uncle Dom's eyes glittered with the anticipation of all that money to be saved. A cold man, the only time I've ever seen him truly happy is when talking about money or receiving Holy Communion. "It's not a complicated process. How large a restaurant are you talking about? Five million a year gross? Ten million a year gross? Two hundred seats, banquet facilities?"

"No, just a small place. Maybe fifty covers?"

The light went out of his eyes. For ten seconds he had thought that I'd seen the error of my ways and was about to play with the big boys.

"Go to a bookstore and buy the Nolo Press book on setting up a corporation in California. It's very well written and concise. Fill out the forms and mail them into Sacramento. You'll be incorporated in no time. A monkey could do it."

I resisted the urge to get up and walk out. I needed some answers and if it meant putting up with Uncle Dom's subtle and not so subtle insults, so be it.

"It can't be that simple," I argued. "Are you telling me that I can buy this book, fill out the forms, and have my mail sent to…to…a taqueria in the Mission? That's it? I'm incorporated?" I said.

"Absolutely. Once incorporated you must return your quarterly forms and be very careful about the taxes," he warned. "That's where they always get you. Other than that, you can set up shop in a dumpster if you wanted."

"What if by some miracle I got the money to open a big place, something about the size of American Fare. Is it a different process?"

"Not really, although the paperwork is considerably more involved. Which is where someone like me comes in. Hmmn, Willie is late, even for him."

While Uncle Dom motioned to Howard and asked him to call the mayor's office for an ETA, I began to put some pieces of the puzzle together. Brent must have gotten the money for the initial start-up costs from Vino Blanco, but for whatever reason, Vino Blanco was not officially in the picture. Why?

"One more question, Uncle Dom. What if I had a silent partner, one that put up the money, but then wasn't involved in anything else beyond that? Doesn't appear on any paperwork, is completely out of the picture. Is that possible?"

"Yes, of course it's possible, but you would have to ask what they are getting in return for their initial investment. No one, no one," he repeated, "does something for nothing."

The sudden rush of waiters to our table signaled the mayor's arrival. Uncle Dom stood up, a not so tacit way of telling me to leave.

"Mary, if you ever want to play with the big money, I'd be happy to help you. This nickel and dime stuff…" he waved his hand dismissively.

"Thanks, Uncle Dom. Give my love to Aunt Mary," I said, but it was lost on him. His attention was fixed on the mayor walking across the dining room to our table.

At the exit I took one last look. Uncle Dom and the mayor tête-à-tête over the menu, a quartet of waiters at the ready. Better them than me.

Chapter 11

I should drink expensive champagne on an empty stomach more often. The stress kinks in my neck had unraveled, and my limbs were heavy with a delicious inertia. I felt mighty fine as I strolled down Montgomery Street toward Embarcadero One where my car was parked. I was toying with the idea of taking a nap in the back seat of my station wagon for a couple of hours when the obsessive, driven part of my personality screamed, "No! You have more questions that need answering."

I bought three Snickers bars and a double espresso from a kiosk on Front Street and wolfed them down. Today's lunch. By the time I reached my car the chocolate and caffeine had kicked in, spoiling the soporific effects of the champagne. My hands were twitching from the caffeine, and the stress kinks were back. No matter.

Time to eat crow.

I drove up Second Street to the alley behind American Fare and parked in the loading zone. I punched in the number to Thom's pager and half-hoped he wouldn't call me back. He was the only one besides Brent who had a total picture of the restaurant's cash flow. I was becoming convinced that Brent was into something illegal, big time illegal, not some measly shakedown of a local purveyor.

I'd give Thom five minutes. If he didn't call me back, then I'd start rifling through the files in the office hoping for some clue.

Thom called me back in four minutes and forty-five seconds.

"Yes," he intoned in a come-hither drawl, elongating both the "Y" and the "S." If his greeting had been any longer I'd have had to buy a Muni Fastpass.

Obviously he didn't recognize the number.

"Thom, it's Mary, Mary Ryan from work."

"Bitch," he yelled into the phone with such ferocity that I almost felt spittle on my cheek.

This was going to be harder than I thought. Grovel, Mary.

"I apologize for my remarks, Thom. I'm *soooo* sorry. You can't imagine how horrible this whole experience has been for me. I lashed out at you because you were there. Please forgive me," I begged. "I want to talk with you about something. I'd be happy to buy you drinks for just a few minutes of your time."

"Drinks? That's all I'm worth? I don't think so, sweetheart. Ta, ta," he trilled.

"Okay, lunch," I said quickly before he hung up.

Silence.

"Some place nice."

Silence again. He was weighing his options. Free lunch with Mary versus stale breadsticks and the dried orange that had been sitting on his counter for a week.

"How nice?" he countered.

"Uh, Rose Pistola?"

"No, I ate there last week. Some place *nice*." It was an order.

The emphasis in his voice signaled major credit card time. Okay, I had just paid off my cards and could afford a little debt.

"Look, *you* choose. You're doing me a favor," I reminded him.

"Let's see," he murmured. I could almost hear the dollar signs chinging in his head. "Waves. I haven't had my protein today. Meet you there in one hour. Don't be late," he ordered.

Sigh.

Very expensive crow.

Waves has the best fish in town and the most unbelievable prices. I've been in the business for fifteen years and still it amazes me what some restaurants charge for their food and what people are willing to pay.

Christ, I'd have to get some clothes. Even with my stratospheric level of chutzpah, I didn't have the nerve to eat there in a ten-year-old Gap tee shirt.

I tore back down Second Street to the Embarcadero. Parked. Found an Ann Taylor. Ordered the saleswoman to find me something in black, size ten, with earrings and shoes to match. I didn't even look at the price tags, just handed her my credit card. I rummaged around in my backpack and found my emergency lipstick. Unfortunately, my emergency mascara had dried up. Makeup is not my strong suit.

I was five minutes late.

Thom was already seated, a magnum of Veuve Clicquot at the tableside. A magnum! I had a feeling this bottle wasn't going to taste nearly as good as the one I'd had earlier, since I was paying for it.

"Hello, Thom. I see you've already ordered some champagne."

He stood with a courtesy that took me by surprise and gave me the once over.

"Mary, for once in your life, you look presentable. If I didn't know better, I'd swear you just bought those clothes. Let me help you with your chair."

While scooting myself under the table I surreptitiously checked my cuffs to make sure no tags were showing.

As usual, Thom was groomed with a capital G: linen pants, raw silk jacket, and monogrammed shirt. How could he possibly afford it? I might not dress well, but I know what expensive clothes look like.

Thom caught our waiter's eye and glanced in my direction. Immediately, the waiter filled my glass. I gave Thom a small smile in recognition of his courtesy. Maybe I should give him some slack now and then. I made judgments about people, and then nothing they did ever changed my opinion.

Memo to self: be more tolerant.

"To lunch." Thom held his glass high in a toast. I toasted him back.

"I think I'll start with the caviar toasts, then the seafood napoleon. What about you?"

I looked at the menu. Caviar toasts: $29.95. Seafood napoleon: $35.95. Plus the magnum of champagne.

Memo to self: ask Brent for a big raise.

"I had a late breakfast. I'll pass on the fish and have the vegetarian soufflé." That was only $16.95.

After we'd ordered, Thom made a grand flourish with his napkin before settling it down on his lap. He looked around the dining room, checked out the floral displays, and nudged the carpet with an expensively clad toe. He let out a contented sigh. "This is *exactly* the sort of restaurant Brent should own. Class, class, class."

Another waiter appeared and poured more champagne. Most likely his job was to ensure that everyone's glass was full, all the time. If lunch entrees were $36.95, I didn't even want to see the wine list.

"Notice the service?" Thom was in raptures. "We should bring our wait staff here for a refresher course."

"It's too…stuffy. Brent didn't want formal, Thom. He wanted something eclectic. That's part of American Fare's charm." I scanned the dining room, and as beautiful as this restaurant was, it didn't have the energy of American Fare. It had one sort of clientele, the extremely well heeled.

"Well, it's *my* kind of place." Thom cupped a hand over one side of his mouth and in a mock whisper said, "Did you *see* what they were charging for their appetizers?"

I knew only too well what they were charging. I took a big swig of champagne. There's nothing worse than destroying that smug euphoria you feel with a passel of debt-free credit cards by racking up hundreds of dollars in charges in the space of two hours.

The substantial dent to my pocketbook aside, here was my opportunity to drill Thom about the restaurant's finances.

"Think of their start-up costs for this place and compare it with what Brent needed to open American Fare. And the downtown rents," I reminded him.

"True, but you know restaurants have a shelf life. Good places have a five, seven year heyday. If lucky, they can hold on for another five years. I never thought I'd *see* the day when Trader Vic's closed. But not even Vic's could survive the essentially fickle nature of the dining public. These people are maximizing their lifespan."

The waiter brought Thom his appetizer and filled our glasses again. My stomach rumbled. The champagne, espresso, and Snickers bars hated each other.

Thom began ladling big hunks of crème fraiche on top of the caviar toasts and popping them in his mouth. All conversation had stopped. At this rate I wouldn't get any more information out of him until dessert.

"How did Brent get the capital to open American Fare?" I tried to sound nonchalant.

"Mmnn, don't know," Thom mumbled. Little bits of roe clung to the edges of his mouth. "Family money, I assume." I looked away. Normally I adore caviar, but the thought of fish on top of chocolate made my stomach clench.

Thom didn't know Brent's father worked an oil rig.

"No partner that you know of? Providing cash flow when we run short."

"No. Although between you and me, some months we could use a bailout. I bet *this* restaurant doesn't have a cash flow problem."

The waiter appeared with our entrees. I pushed my soufflé to the side and tried to not panic about losing my job. Was it only yesterday that I was blithely contemplating quitting? What was I thinking? I was a single woman with a mortgage and working for a restaurant that might not make payroll next month. Despite the state of my stomach, I drained my champagne flute.

"Are you telling me American Fare is in financial trouble?" My voice must have been too loud.

"Ssh," he said, his hands fluttering up and down ordering me to be quiet. "You didn't hear it from *my* lips," he back-pedaled. "And it's not really financial trouble. Some months Brent doesn't take a salary to cover payroll."

I didn't bother to hide my astonishment. How could Brent forgo his salary for even one month, never mind several? The house in St. Francis Woods, the expensive clothes, kids in private school, the designer girlfriend. Who was paying for this?

"Why so curious about the restaurant, Mary? What's so important that you'd suffer through lunch with me?" Thom may have been snotty and pretentious, but he wasn't stupid.

Memo to self: stop underrating people.

"I wanted to see how we were financially. I need a new car and was hoping to hit Brent up for a raise." It was shocking at how easily the lie popped out of my mouth.

"Well, having seen that heap you drive, it's about time. However, I wouldn't ask Brent for a raise. If I were you, I'd hold on to that hunk of junk for a while. Brent's very testy these days. A couple of weeks ago I suggested we pare down our wine suppliers to maximize the volume we get from certain brokers to get bigger discounts. You'd think he'd have gotten down on his knees and thanked me for trying to improve the restaurant's cash flow. Let me tell you, he went *berserk*, yelling at me that we weren't to change anything to do with the wine. Then he *stomped* out of the office. Thank God, Juan was there. He ran after him and calmed him down. Brent apologized later. I was just doing my job," Thom sniffed.

Was Brent shaking down one of our wine brokers?

"Which brokers did you want to cut?" I asked casually and took a bite of my soufflé in an attempt to calm my stomach.

"I thought we'd start out by consolidating a couple of the Australian brokers, and Juan assured me he'd negotiate with the South American brokers to get a better pricing structure. You know how corrupt it is down there. Twenty bribes before it even leaves the country."

Thom's plate was clean. My soufflé sat mostly untouched despite the mambo going on in my stomach. I couldn't eat another bite. Between the two of us, the magnum was almost empty. I'd never felt more sober in my life.

Chapter 12

I might not have been drunk, but by the end of the meal I had a hangover. Thom insisted on ordering dessert and an espresso. The dessert menu consisted of those structural confections that Thom adores and is always nagging me to put on our menu. A chunk of chocolate covered with ice cream flew across the table as Thom tried to cut into his dessert and landed on the arm of my new outfit. On top of the charges for the clothes, lunch, and parking, I now had a dry cleaning bill.

At the end of the meal, Thom insisted on paying the tip.

"Mary, that was lovely. I must pay the tip. No arguments. And don't worry about American Fare. That was the champagne talking. Let's do this again. Soon. Next time, my treat. You know, given half a chance, I think we could be good friends. We have the same snide sense of humor. And I mean that as a compliment."

He was so sincere I blushed. I had wooed someone I made no secret of despising with food and champagne to divulge information about American Fare we both knew was none of my business, and here he was thanking me profusely for my lies and treachery.

Memo to self: really work on your intolerance.

My headache was so intense that I went straight to bed when I got home. Carlos' funeral was the next morning and I wanted to be on time. I still had a headache when I got up the next morning. I wasn't sure if it was champagne or angst. I tried to ignore the tom-tom of worry beating in the back of my head.

You have a thirty-year mortgage and drive a fifteen-year-old car with one hundred and twenty thousand miles on it. You are single. You are the breadwinner. And your employer might not make payroll next month.

Of course, it wasn't that dire. I could always borrow money from my parents if I needed to, plus I had a fair amount in savings, but never since my divorce had I felt so vulnerable. So alone.

Arriving early, I found the church almost empty except for the ubiquitous old ladies dressed in black from head to toe hunched over their rosary beads. It was so familiar and soothing that my headache disappeared.

This was one of those glorious old-fashioned churches they don't build anymore; its ceilings arched forever, its niches graced with the obligatory, oddly touching religious statues. The altar and pews were bathed in red and blue light from the ornate stained glass windows above. If I'd been born in the Middle Ages I probably would have been a nun. As a child the beauty of the art, architecture, and music of the Catholic Church seduced me. I stayed in the church for many years after my faith had lapsed because I so loved singing in the church choir.

I stood just inside the door, savoring the old-fashioned majesty of the nave, until I saw O'Connor's broad back in the corner of the last pew. Seeing him sitting there with the intention of waylaying me made me all the more determined to avoid him as long as possible. I veered off to left and took the side aisle up to the front. I ignored his heavy warning coughs coming from the back of the church. If O'Connor wanted to see me he could come get me.

Out of habit I lit a candle for Carlos and sat down in the fourth row, the first three rows being reserved for family. Ten minutes later I saw a young, pregnant woman in a voluminous black veil and dress herd three children into the front pew. Carlos' widow. Slowly, the church began filling up, the monotonous shuffling of feet, the clunk of the kneelers as they hit the floor, and the ill-timed chatter of children and their mothers hushing them, sounds that precede every mass.

Right before the mass started, someone sat down next to me and touched my sleeve. Expecting O'Connor, I was pleasantly surprised to see Juan. I turned to him and whispered, "Thanks so much for calling everyone. I really appreciate it."

"*De nada*," he whispered back and then put a finger up to his lips as the priests marched to the altar to begin Carlos' funeral.

The mass was in Spanish, but the cues were the same. I effortlessly crossed myself, stood, and knelt at the appropriate times. Mesmerized by the ritualistic beauty of the mass, I felt calm for the first time in days. I hoped Carlos' wife derived comfort from this ritual. I envy people who have faith. In some ways it's so simple. You believe and assume God will provide. Although atheism is intellectual high ground, heathens like me are a little bereft when, say, your husband leaves you or you find someone strangled in a linen closet.

Once we filed out of the church, I made a beeline for the bathroom in an effort to ditch O'Connor. When I came out fifteen minutes later the hall was filled to capacity. Long tables had been pushed against the perimeter of the room and volunteers were setting up the food. The atmosphere reminded me of an Irish wake. People were talking loudly and children were playing tag, the boisterous voices in strange contrast to the somber clothing.

Knowing I'd have to talk to Carlos' wife, I stood for what seemed like forever in a receiving line. The veil was gone, and her dress strained across her stomach with a sort of last-minute-need-a-black-dress Salvation Army feel to it. Her face, anguished but polite, had that angelic and vulnerable expression of the statues upstairs. The weariness of her shoulders and the visible effort she was making to keep her back and her face straight convinced me this woman knew nothing about her husband's death. She looked battered by grief.

Finally it was my turn. Not knowing the extent of her English, I shook her hand and said simply, "Hello, Mrs. Perez, I'm so sorry about Carlos. I really liked working with him. I'm Mary."

I could tell at first she thought I was some sort of nameless prep cook who worked with Carlos, but when she heard my name her face became animated. She said slowly, "Wait, *Señora*," and held her hand up in the air in an effort to reiterate she didn't want me to go. She fired off something in Spanish to the person next to her, who then ran off. A ten-year-old boy came running up and started speaking to her very quickly in Spanish. She replied, then he turned to me and said in English, "Mrs. Perez wants you to come to her house at four today, after the reception. She wants to talk with you."

Great. My face must have shown my reluctance because she grabbed my hand with one of her heavily gloved black ones and squeezed it. She looked at me very intensely and begged, "Please," those Madonna-like eyes pleading with me. The wimp in me nodded. The little boy gave me the address, and I promised I would be there.

I glanced over at the food table to see if any lines had started forming. Not yet. God, I was starving. Out of the corner of one eye I saw O'Connor up against the wall watching me. He crooked his finger and beckoned me to him. It would have been childish to refuse.

Crossing the hall, I stood next to him, my chin high, my fists clenched. I was ready for battle.

"I'm sorry about Saturday night, Mary. I'm real worried I'm going to be removed from this case. I lashed out at you. Christ knows you don't need that right now."

My combative stance melted with every word. "It's all right," I mumbled. "What do you mean, they're going to take you off the case?"

"You have to admit, I'm not exactly in an unbiased position here. The captain is aware of our relationship and has given me a week to solve this case, then it goes to someone else."

"R-r-relationship?" I felt myself blush.

"Jim, me, you. The captain doesn't like it. He doesn't like the fact you discovered the body. The only thing that's keeping me on so far is the violence of the murder. Once he got the autopsy report, he ruled you out as a suspect. Perez was beaten to a pulp before he was strangled. No one in their right mind could see a woman inflicting that much damage."

We were both silent. Carlos' poor mangled face loomed large in my mind. I hugged myself tightly.

I cleared my throat. "O'Connor, I want to apologize, too. I didn't thank you for bringing dinner. It was very thoughtful of you."

O'Connor shrugged and smiled. "Forget it." Then he became all business. "What's the scoop on these people. Are most of them from the restaurant?"

"Well, all the Latinos who work in the restaurant are here. Some of the others, too, but a lot of people I don't know." I looked around the hall one more time. That's strange, I thought, Brent's not here, nor Amos or Thom. "I haven't seen Gilberto, if that's what you're hinting at. He wasn't in the church as far as I know, and I haven't seen him down here either. O'Connor, he didn't kill his own brother. I know these guys."

He sighed. "Mary, you don't know what goes on in people's lives. You see them at work, maybe at a few parties. Do you think that makes you an authority? I've known your husband most of my life. I never would've believed he'd leave you for another woman."

That shut me up.

"I won't learn anything here. If Perez shows up, page me right away. Here's my business card."

"I'll keep my eyes open," I promised.

"Call me when you get home and let me know what your impressions are," he said, sounding brusque and official. He left the hall, his broad back stiff with authority.

Lines for the food were finally starting to form. The utilitarian tables from the church were groaning under the weight of brightly painted platters piled high with Salvadoran delicacies. Three dishwashers from the restaurant began instructing me as to which fruit drinks were spiked with booze, which foods were laced with hot peppers, what to eat with fingers. We laughed over my ignorance, and I could tell they enjoyed playing teacher for a change. Aside from the fact that we were all wearing black, a casual observer would have thought this was a big party.

We were having a good time until Juan appeared. Unfortunately, he was back in Uriah Heep mode. The others just sort of drifted away, and I found myself alone with him, as he clucked and hovered over me like a mother hen. He refilled my plate after I'd taken only three bites, refreshed my drink when I'd barely touched it. He apologized again and again for his behavior with the wine delivery guy.

After about twenty minutes I couldn't stand it anymore. Having dutifully checked out everyone's general reactions, I didn't think anything was amiss. I said my good-byes as gracefully as possible and exited the hall. I was shocked that Brent hadn't showed up. Carlos might never have advanced beyond being a prep cook, but he deserved some recognition by the boss, even if it was only at his own funeral.

When I left the church hall it was noon. Because I didn't have to be at Carlos' place until four, I decided to head downtown to Nordstrom to buy a new outfit. When I got there I took a really hard look at myself for the first time in months. The dressing room mirror reflected the worn-out shell of the woman I used to be. In addition to my being borderline anorexic, my skin had a sickly cast to it, indicating a serious vitamin deficiency—not surprising considering my eating habits of late. My hair, streaked with gray, was the color of three-day-old liver—another hint I wasn't getting enough nutrients.

In horror, I ran to the spa and got a massage, makeover, manicure, and a decent haircut and a rinse. Two hours later, the gray had been replaced by a sexy, mahogany sheen, my fingers and toes were apple red, and all my limbs felt as limp as overcooked pasta. Fighting the urge to check into a hotel and sleep until morning, I fortified myself with a double espresso from the coffee bar and dragged myself back down to the Mission.

Carlos' family lived in a third-floor railroad flat on 16th near Sanchez. Forcing my rubbery legs to negotiate the treacherous stairwell, I thought of Carlos' heavily pregnant wife corralling three kids up these stairs three and four times a day. She must have been waiting for me because she opened the door before I had a chance to knock.

"Mrs. Perez." I held out my hand.

She took my hand and squeezed it. "Rosa, *por favor.*"

She led me inside and, with a wave of her hand, indicated an orange Naugahyde recliner for me to sit in. The decor in the apartment certainly explained why Carlos sported such weird haircuts. He'd had a real sense of the extreme. He had combed local flea markets for furniture and then painted everything in a riot of bright reds, oranges, and turquoises. For the *pièce-de-résistance*, the walls were a bright lemon yellow. The room was overcrowded and tacky, but also vibrant and joyous. It would be impossible to be depressed in such a room.

The apartment was quiet. Too quiet. No kids. No little boy to interpret. Rosa had changed out of her ill-fitting black mourning dress into a maternity muumuu. That ramrod stance she'd maintained in the reception hall had broken, and she had big circles under her eyes. Once nestled in the corner of a lime-green overstuffed couch, she mutely canvassed my new haircut, makeup, and nails. I could feel my face flame bell-pepper red with embarrassment.

"*Los niños?*" I asked, both to break the ice and take her mind off my ill-timed makeover.

"My sister's," she said slowly.

Leaning forward she said in very halting English, "Carlos good husband. I good wife. Carlos in something bad. At restaurant, something bad, something *malo*."

"What was *malo?*" I asked.

She shrugged her shoulders, her frustration evident. "No tell me, I know bad. Help me. You know?"

Again, I cursed my laziness in not learning basic Spanish. She repeated the same phases over and over again, finishing with, "Please *Señora*, Carlos like you, he trust you. Help me."

I looked at her in desperation. "I'm sorry, I know nothing." I suggested, "The *policia...?*"

With that universal dismissal by Latinos of official authority, she made a move as if to spit, her contempt plain. "No, *Señora*. You find out. For me, *por favor*," she begged, her hands held out in supplication.

Completely in the dark as to what she was talking about, I tried another angle. "Rosa, do you think Gilberto killed Carlos? Nobody has seen him. Do you know where he is?"

"Gilberto no kill Carlos," she said emphatically. "Gilberto good man. Like Carlos. No kill Carlos, *Señora*."

"Do you know where Gilberto is? You must tell me. I know Gilberto would never hurt Carlos, but the police don't know that. He's got to come forward before they find him first. Please, where is he?"

I heard the soft padding of sneakers and turned my head. Gilberto came into the room and sat down beside Rosa on the couch.

Of the two brothers, I knew Carlos much better. Gilberto was also a hard worker, but overshadowed by his wisecracking, happy-go-lucky brother. As lean as his brother was stocky, Gilberto had lost about ten pounds and aged five years in the last three days. Resisting the impulse to hug him, I waited for him to make the first move.

He stared me full in the face and with no hesitation stated, "I didn't kill my brother, *Señora*."

"Gilberto, I know you didn't kill Carlos. I've told the police that over and over, but they don't believe me. You must understand, your disappearance is very suspicious. It looks like you killed Carlos and then fled. You need to talk with them yourself."

"I can't." He sounded angry and frustrated.

"Why not?" I implored.

No answer.

"Please, Gilberto, please, call this man." I handed him O'Connor's card. "He's a police officer, but he's a good friend of mine and will listen to you. Turn yourself in before they find you," I pleaded.

He turned the card over in his hands a few times and then crushed it in his fist. "I can't. There's a lot you don't understand. I had nothing to do with his killing, but I can't go to the police."

"Does it have to do with the restaurant? What's going on there?"

He shot Rosa a look and asked her a bunch of questions in rapid-fire Spanish. She answered back with a defiant tone in her voice. Soon they were having a rip-roaring fight. Their words were bouncing off each other like water on a hot griddle. Although I couldn't understand what they were saying, clearly she wasn't going to back down. She ended the fight by turning away from him and cocooning herself in a corner of the couch.

Gilberto turned to me. "Nothing's going on there, *Señora*. Nothing." He shot Rosa a stern look. "You stay away from the restaurant for a few days."

"Gilberto, why should I stay away from the restaurant if nothing's going on there?"

"You listen to me. Stay away from there," he ordered, his voice hoarse with emotion.

Rosa obviously understood English better than she could speak it, because she responded to his comments with a few choice sentences that made Gilberto's jaw clench even harder. She then turned to me and, with her chin high with defiance, begged, "Please help me, *Señora*."

Well, there was no pleasing both of them. I said ambiguously, "I'll do what I can. Gilberto, are you going to go the police?"

He shook his head vehemently no. Short of turning him in, I couldn't do anything more. I prayed they didn't find him first.

"Do you need any money?" I asked gently.

He shrugged in that noncommittal Latin way. I fished into my wallet for the hundred-dollar bill I keep hidden in case of emergency. I got up and tucked the money into his shirt pocket. I put my hand on his shoulder.

"Do you have my phone number?"

He nodded and then repeated it from memory.

"Call me if you need anything. Okay?"

He turned his face away from me, his shoulders curved toward each other to hide the tears on his cheeks. I gave his shoulder a squeeze and put on my coat.

"I need to go now," I said to Rosa. "I'll be in touch if I find out anything."

Rosa used both hands to extract herself from the sofa, came over to me and hugged me, whispering, "*Gracias, muchas gracias.*"

As I headed out the front door Gilberto called out after me, "*Señora*, be careful, *por favor*. Very careful."

The second I shut the door I heard them renewing their argument.

I hit rush hour in full swing. It took me forty-five minutes just to get on the freeway. As I inched my way up the on-ramp, I thought about the events of the past four days: Brent stealing files from his own restaurant; Teri Baxter's confession about Brent's skullduggery; discovering the phantom owner of American Fare; Rosa's desperate plea to help find Carlos' killer; Gilberto and Rosa's fight; and, most puzzling of all, Gilberto's refusal to speak to the police, despite his protests of innocence.

I'd been so engrossed in trying to catalogue everything that I'd neglected to keep my eyes open for the blue van. It wasn't until I finally got on the bridge that I remembered to check my rearview mirror. There it was, two lanes over and three cars behind. Again, I tried to pooh-pooh my suspicions, telling myself that every fourth family in the United States had one of these vans. In my gut I knew that van was following me.

I pushed the Subaru up to speeds and maneuvers worthy of Steve McQueen and *Bullitt*. People honked, flipped me off, and made every obscene gesture imaginable. I lost sight of him around the tollbooths. Instead of taking the Berkeley curve like I normally do, I went out West Grand and took side streets home.

I arrived home around six, my whole body screaming for a hot shower. Sitting in traffic with the sun beating down on me had practically enameled fifty dollars' worth of Lancôme to my face. My neck and back were one gigantic itch, as stray hairs from the haircut crawled down my back.

First I'd get these clothes off my back and call O'Connor with a progress report on the funeral and my mysterious van driver. Then I was going to take a long, hot shower to wash away my feeble attempts at glamour.

The reason why Brent didn't attend Carlos' funeral was all too apparent when I entered my bedroom. He lay on my bed, dead from a bullet hole through his head.

Chapter 13

I knew Brent was dead; no one who loses that much blood is alive. He was sprawled on top of one of my prized possessions, a Texas star quilt Jim and I'd bought on our honeymoon in New Orleans. Even in the dusky light, the bright yellows, pinks, and greens were garish against the dark stain of his blood. He'd shot himself in the head; the gun rested quietly in his open hand.

I called 911 and paced around the house, frantically looking for something to do with my hands. The cops who arrived on the scene found me in the kitchen making brioche.

They led me into the living room and told me to sit on the couch. Before they began their barrage of questions, I told them to call O'Connor, he was connected with the case. One of them beeped O'Connor on a cell phone and the preliminary questioning began. No, I'd no idea why he was in my bedroom with a bullet through his brain. No, I wasn't here when he shot himself, I was at a funeral.

In the background I heard the thump of police shoes on my hardwood floors and blinked in reflex from the occasional flash of the cameras as they catalogued Brent's final pose and the meager contents of my bedroom. I saw how stark my life would look once those pictures were developed: old catalogues strewn haphazardly on the floor by the bed, no pictures on the walls, the dingy paint job.

I tuned out the questions and started quietly crying, playing and replaying that bleak and lonely newsreel in my head. Not two days ago I was sneering at Teri Baxter for her gadget-filled concrete bunker, but at least she was reaching out in her limited way for something to touch her. I'd lived here an entire year and the only things in the house that reflected my personality were an espresso machine, a Kitchen Aid mixer, an ice cream maker, ten copper pots, enough wire whips, wooden spoons, and spatulas to outfit a small restaurant, and a quilt soaked with Brent's blood.

Brent was essentially a shallow, insecure man, who in an effort to prove he wasn't a hick often showed up at work in the most outlandish Italian couture. But put the man in a kitchen and all his insecurity melted away. I've never worked with someone who was so excited about the entire experience of dining. Sometimes I'd go to the produce market just to hear him shout with glee when he'd find the perfect green beans or the ripest strawberries. Once in the kitchen, cleaning, chopping, and sautéing those green beans was almost a religious experience. He was the first chef in San Francisco to open up the kitchen so diners could actually see people cooking. Sometimes he'd put tables in the kitchen, unifying the chef and the patron, serving up those beans right from the sauté pan to the dinner plate.

Images of Brent passed through my mind: scouring the farms of Sonoma for the freshest goat cheese; chortling with pleasure when drinking a fine Bordeaux; eating the first ripe peaches of the season, the juice running down his chin. And the final image, Brent dead in my bedroom, his brains curdled all over my pillows. I sobbed even harder.

I don't know how long I lay in a ball on the sofa whimpering and crying. When it finally played itself out, I opened my eyes to see O'Connor sitting across from me with a cup of coffee in his hand.

"Do you want something to drink?" he asked grimly.

I nodded.

"Let's go into the kitchen to wash your face first. You look like hell."

He motioned the cop standing next to him to follow us into the kitchen. He wasn't kidding. Catching myself in the dining room mirror, I saw that my crying jag had loosened all that expensive makeup. The beiges, pinks, greens, and browns were running down my face in variegated stripes. The espresso machine hissed and chortled in the background while I scrubbed my face clean until it was parched from the dish soap.

After I dried my face on a dishtowel, O'Connor led me into the living room and stood by the front door.

"Here you go," he said, handing me a warm mug of milk. He probably thought my stomach couldn't handle any coffee. He was right. Holding the door open with his other hand, he gestured me outside. "Let's go talk in my car. Give the guys some room to maneuver."

We walked out to his car and sat down in the front seat. We didn't say anything for about ten minutes. I was shivering, from shock I suppose, and the warmth of the milk and the heat from his car seats made me feel a whole lot better. I finished my milk and turned to face him. His hands were in his lap, clenched into fat, mean fists.

"Ryan, this isn't good. I brought you out here for two reasons. One, I want them to search your house without you in there potentially destroying or concealing evidence. They found some men's clothing hung up in your closet with Brent's initials monogrammed on them and men's toiletries in your bathroom. This obviously implicates you in whatever happened in there."

I stared at him in disbelief and started to exit the car. I wanted to see this for myself. He grabbed my wrist, hard. If I'd struggled with him he would have broken it. I shut the door with my free hand and relaxed. He let go. The milk started churning in my stomach, and I thought I was going to be sick for the second time in four days.

"My God, O'Connor, you can't think I would have anything to do with Brent. What with Jim and everything, I couldn't possibly, I just...." I could feel myself starting to get hysterical, not even speaking in sentences, but throwing out words and phrases like, "betrayed," "couldn't even think about," "hating everything and everyone," rambling on and on about me, Jim, and my deep unhappiness after the divorce.

Reminiscent of my scene with Teri, O'Connor broke the fit by taking my chin in one of his humongous hands and forcing me to make eye contact with him. After locking eyes for a long moment, I broke away. Crouching into a ball, I glued myself to the door, the L-shaped handle digging a big bruise in my back I'd have for days.

"You okay?" O'Connor asked gently.

I nodded.

"I want to hear your story privately. I know you, and I find it damn near impossible to believe you were having an affair with Brown. For one thing, you're too old. From what you've told me, all his affairs haven't been a day over twenty-five."

"Thanks a lot." I thought about all that gray in my hair before my makeover.

"Age has its privileges in this case. Be grateful you don't fit the bill. For another, I know you've been pretty busted up over your divorce. Now, I want you to tell me everything you did from the time you discovered Perez until now."

I told him everything, well, almost everything. I didn't mention seeing Gilberto at the paint store or at Rosa's apartment. He hadn't killed Carlos.

"Did you have any idea that the restaurant was in financial shit?"

"No, Brent never said anything to me about watching my food cost. Looks where he lives...lived. His kids go to private schools. He drives, drove a Porsche. I thought we were raking it in."

"What was the address of that taqueria?"

"I can't remember exactly. It's on Mission between 16th and 17th. There's no sign and the awning is in shreds. Just look for the guy with the cleaver aimed at your head."

O'Connor smacked my arm. "Would you be serious?"

I stared out the window, trying to swallow the hysteria welling up inside.

"If I don't make jokes I'm going to lose it."

O'Connor took my hands, which were clutched together in front of my chin as if I was praying, and one by one unfurled them from each other and placed them in my lap.

"You're doing fine. Keep it together, Mary. Look at me. Do you feel better?"

I swallowed a couple of times and nodded.

"Good," he answered. "Now, let's act as if they aren't going to charge you with anything just yet...."

"Charge me!" My voice reverberated throughout the car.

"Hold on." He held up both hands to stop my impending hysteria. "It looks like suicide. They'll proceed along those lines. Until we get the report back pinpointing the time of death, we'll count you out initially since you were at the funeral most of the morning. Now what did you do between the time you left the church and met with Mrs. Perez?"

My face went beet red. I cursed myself for having that makeover. I mumbled, "I went to Nordstrom and got a make-over and a massage."

"Thank God. You'll be in their books and people will remember you. Good thing you didn't just shop around. On the surface it looks like you were getting it on the side with Brown, something went wrong, and he killed himself in your bed. Or you got jealous and killed him. Fine, I know different. I privately plan to treat this as a murder by persons unknown. Which in my gut I know it is. Publicly, I'll go along with the party line."

"Privately? Publicly?" I sing-songed in confusion.

"Mary, you're connected with two bodies in four days. If the coroner rules it's murder, you're in big trouble. The first person they'll look at is you. I don't know why you've been singled out, but someone is trying to set you up. I'm fighting like hell to stay on the case, but if your alibi doesn't hold up, the captain's yanking me as of five minutes ago. We've gotta move fast. When they take you downtown, tell the truth. Don't hide anything. Keep reiterating you don't know how Brown's clothes got into your bedroom, you've got no idea why he decided to commit suicide in your house. Be very firm and confident in your replies."

"I'll try, but it's going to sound ridiculous."

"I realize that. Tell me about your neighbors. Is anyone likely to have been home today?"

I mentally catalogued my neighbors: all young lawyers and stockbrokers eager to start families and take advantage of the Albany School District. "Not really. Most of the old people have died off and have been replaced by couples who both work."

"Too bad. The same thing's happening in my neighborhood. I went to two funerals last month. Is that it?"

"Your only hope is Mr. Mulliken, the guy two doors down and across the street. He's bedridden and sleeps most of the day, but you could try him. His bedroom faces the street. Also, he gets Meals on Wheels. Maybe the driver saw something."

"Good, that gives us something to work with. I'll call you after I tell Mrs. Brown the news. Come right home after you make your statement and we'll touch base. Okay?"

"His kids…," I muttered.

"His kids. It's the shits. Sometimes I hate my job." He cleared his throat. "I'm sorry about Brown. I know you worked with him a long time."

"Yeah, I did." I felt myself getting weepy again and concentrated on the sun visor in an effort not to cry.

"Mary, come on. I need you hitting on all four right now. Whether you realize it or not, you're my best resource. You know the people and the setup."

I took a deep breath and faced him. He looked so tired, his olive, black Irish complexion gray with fatigue. "I'm all right now."

"First, I can't take your official statement. It's got to be someone else, someone you don't know. I called the captain and he's having a couple of new detectives that aren't connected with Jim or me meet you at the station to get your statement. If it starts to get ugly, don't take any shit, demand a lawyer. Call your Uncle Dom. Got it?"

I nodded, but knew that they would have to be shoving hot pokers under my nails before I'd call my uncle to counsel me on beating a murder rap.

"I'm watching your back and mine. My friendship with you is now working against us. I've got to treat Brown's death with kid gloves until we establish you an alibi. Now, do you have it together to go downtown?"

"I guess so." I began chewing my lips, something I did only in times of severe stress. A battle waged inside of me. Should I tell him about Gilberto? O'Connor was bending God knows how many rules on my behalf and I wasn't coming clean with him.

"Uh, do you guys have any leads on Gilberto Perez?"

"No. He didn't show at the funeral. Bet he was here doing in Brown."

I rolled my eyes. "Oh for Christ's sake, O'Connor. Do you really think he's sophisticated enough to simulate Brent's suicide? How would he get Brent's things into my house?"

"Maybe not, but he's not alone on this one. Mary, everything about this case has an organized feel to it, from putting the body in the bag, which obviously was going to be hauled out the door at some point, to planting Brent's possessions in your house. I've put an APB out for Perez's arrest. He might be a small fish in the bigger picture, but I gotta start somewhere."

Flying in the face of everything I'd learned being a cop's wife, I went with my gut. That kid didn't kill anyone. Gilberto seemed frustrated and angry, not remorseful or defensive.

No, I'd wait until I found out what time Brent was killed. If it happened around four o'clock, then Gilberto would have an airtight alibi. If Brent had been killed much earlier, I'd have to turn him in.

"Something else, O'Connor. I think someone's following me. There's been a late model blue van trailing me off and on for the last two days."

He paused for a couple of seconds and shifted uneasily in his seat. "Mary, you've been through a lot the last couple of days. I own one of those vans myself. Do you really think someone has been following you?"

Putting my fears into words made me feel silly and neurotic. O'Connor's reaction didn't do anything to allay my insecurities. I shrugged, "No, I guess not."

I reached for the door handle, then stopped. "O'Connor, two things: first, keep Jim away from me. I don't want any phone calls or visits."

"That's going to be tough, Ryan." Shaking his head, he ran his big hands through his black hair. He was going gray, too.

"I don't care how you do it, keep him away from me. I can't handle him on top of everything else." I looked O'Connor in the eye and placed my soap-parched hand on his thick shoulder. "Second, don't risk your career for me."

He flashed me a grin. "Mary, the Irish have to stick together, you know that."

Chapter 14

Now I know how all those criminals on the news feel when they're being hauled away. Fortunately it was dark by the time we drove to the police station. My neighbors were huddled together in tight-knit groups just outside the crime-scene tape, no doubt comparing notes on my lack of general civility. The last year had been one long lost weekend for me, and I hadn't said anything more than a curt hello to anyone. Frankly, I didn't need to hear about their wonderful marriages and plans for children when I'd just lost all hope of both.

I was spared the indignity of being driven away in a police car. Because of the connection with Carlos' murder, S.F.P.D. pulled rank. One of the sergeants from the scene drove me in my car to San Francisco to make my statement. It was a long silent drive, punctuated only by the sergeant slipping my clutch every time he downshifted. I'd just had that clutch replaced six months ago. I might as well have burned six hundred dollars in the ashtray.

I thought I knew every inspector in homicide, either by name or reputation, but the two detectives who interviewed me were strangers. They must have been recently promoted. One was a short, stout Latina named Chavez who obviously spent a hefty sum on her dry cleaning. Her blouse was so starched it hung off her shoulders in stiff salute. The other detective was a tall, muscular black guy named Porter whose street-smart, lazy body language fooled me into thinking, oh-oh, quota time. Then he opened his mouth and right away I kicked myself for being so racist.

I spent the next two hours responding to the same questions over and over again asked in slightly different ways. No, I didn't know why Chef Brown blew his brains out in my bedroom. No, we weren't having an affair. Yes, we did work together for over seven years, but our relationship was strictly platonic. Yes, I do live alone. No, I didn't know why men's clothes and toiletries were in my house. No, I didn't know whose they were. No, they do not belong to my ex-husband. By the end of the session I'd chewed my lips to a pulp.

Several times during the questioning I almost broke down and called Uncle Dom. It was a toss-up which was more terrifying, facing a potential murder charge or my uncle. As it was, the fallout from Brent's body being found at my house was going to be huge.

Tomorrow morning Uncle Dom would return from six o'clock Mass. He'd pick up the *San Francisco Chronicle* that my aunt places exactly four inches from his coffee cup. On the front page would be his niece's name in bold, black type being tied to a murder investigation. At precisely 7:01 he'd call me and the real interrogation would begin.

In the end I decided to take my chances with Inspectors Chavez and Porter. S.F.P.D. would be a piece of cake compared to Uncle Dom.

Finally they gave each other some secret signal. Porter switched off the tape recorder. Chavez stood up and politely reminded me I might be needed for further questioning once the lab reports on the body were back. I reassured them I'd let Inspector O'Connor know my whereabouts at all times. As I walked down the hall, I felt their eyes following me out the door, every step scrutinized. Despite their courteous manner, I sensed they were like dogs panting to attack and frustrated by an imaginary leash.

It was nine when I exited the station. I felt like a homeless person. Even though Brent must have been on his way to an autopsy by now, I didn't want to go home until a cleaning service had mopped up the blood and residue from the print powder. With disgust, I recalled how the restaurant looked after Carlos' murder.

So exhausted that my eyes were beginning to cross, I didn't trust myself to negotiate the bridge. Nor did I want to be there tomorrow morning when Uncle Dom started his barrage of phone calls. I decided to spend the night in one of those utilitarian motels on Lombard Street, the kind with the tired and tacky coffee shops and the waitresses that call you "hon." I'd get something to eat, go to bed, and then return to the East Bay in the morning.

I got my car out of the police garage, drove down to Van Ness, followed Van Ness to Lombard, and turned into the first motel with a lit vacancy sign. Something important nagged at me in the back of my mind, but try as I might, I couldn't remember what it was.

I took a long shower, put my suit back on, and went to the coffee shop for a quick bite to eat. After downing a grease-laden, thoroughly enjoyable plate of sausages, scrambled eggs, and hash browns, I returned to my room. It was ten, just about my bedtime, but the food had given me a second wind. I didn't want to turn on the television; I'd had enough sensory overload for one day. I'd clean my purse, a woman's last anti-dote to boredom.

Dumping out everything on the bed, I methodically picked through all the loose pieces of paper. I checked the scraps over to see if any of them were important. Often when I see an unusual presentation or a great dessert, I'll jot down the information on napkins or old receipts, anything I can find. Consequently, my purse is always filled with tiny miscellaneous bit of paper with recipes and drawings on them. Most chefs are food vultures. I know one highly regarded chef who eats out three times a week to see what the competition is doing and to "borrow" any interesting ideas.

One piece of paper caught my eye immediately; American Fare's logo was on top. It was the paper on which I'd written down the addresses of Brent's girlfriends: Teri Baxter and Drew Smyth-Sommers. Hot dog, Drew's address was in the Marina on Scott Street, two blocks away from my motel.

Despite the late hour, I walked down Scott to find myself at a very elegant three-story townhouse painted white with black lacquer trim. Blood-red begonias cascaded out of blue-and-white Chinese porcelain pots on small balconies below the floor-to-ceiling windows. Money and class in spades. She wasn't going to be a pushover like poor Teri Baxter.

I fetched a comb from my purse and ran it through my damp hair while I crunched an Altoid. I rang the front doorbell. Even her door chimes sounded expensive.

Luckily Drew was home. As she opened the door, clouds of *Joy* billowed out the door, filling my mouth and nose with its overpowering scent. The heavy perfume mixed with the remnants of the Altoid made me gag a little.

Drew was decked out in scandalously expensive ice-blue lounging pajamas the exact color of her eyes, and her feet were daintily shod in white silk mules with her initials embroidered on them. Seeing her standing there in the soft glow of the porch light looking like a photo out of Vogue made me feel like some Appalachian coal miner's daughter wearing a dress made from flour sacks.

My linen suit, the epitome of chic at nine o'clock this morning, looked like I'd slept in it for a couple of days. I glanced down at my black pumps, scuffed on the toes. Her perfume reminded me I wasn't even wearing deodorant, and I didn't dare sneak a peek to see if my blouse front was clean. I was at a decided tactical disadvantage.

I took a deep breath and started gushing hellos and how-are-you's. Her response was a guarded, "Fine." With a lizard-like calm, she waited for me to explain my business.

"Drew, I was in the neighborhood and just decided to drop by. I wondered if you were, ah, sick or something, I didn't see you at Carlos' funeral." I tried to sound solicitous.

"No," she said, with a tasteful tinge of remorse. "I had another appointment, unfortunately. I sent flowers." Switching gears, she continued in a decidedly dismissive tone, "I'll see you at the restaurant. Sorry I can't stop to chat, I was just getting into bed. Good night."

Yeah, right. Every night before I go to bed I pour half a bottle of $100-an-ounce perfume on me, too. Who was she waiting for?

I had other plans.

I'd already maneuvered my foot between the door and the jamb, and as she began to shut the door, assuming our little encounter was over, she crushed my foot. I screamed loud enough to make her think she'd hurt me. I clutched my foot and leaned against the doorjamb, my eyes closed as if in great pain.

"Oh, my God," she sputtered. "Are you all right?" I took guilty pleasure in seeing her eternal calm shattered for once.

"Yes, I think so. May I come in and sit down for a minute?" All those manners drummed into me by the nuns were finally paying off.

I didn't wait for her to reply. I pushed past her, edged myself along the wall, and sat down on the staircase leading up to her place. Rubbing my ankle vigorously, I said with a wan smile, "I won't be long, it's feeling a little better already."

Resignation on her face, she asked politely, "Would you like something to drink?"

"Oh, just some water, please. That would be great."

I watched her lithe figure glide up the stairs, her mules making a harsh flap-flap sound on the hardwood.

Brent and Drew had been an item for about a year. She's the classic Brent girlfriend, about as removed from his sarcastic, obese wife as possible. In another era she'd have been one of those movie goddesses with a full-length mink slung casually over her shoulders, regardless of the weather. A woman always cold to the touch. Beautiful in a chilly Grace Kelly sort of way, her blue eyes registering only two emotions: disdain and boredom. Why Brent was attracted to her was beyond me.

I suspected she worked in the restaurant because (a) she's the type of person who needs to be at the center of whatever scene is current, and American Fare is very much the scene in San Francisco; and (b) she has a thing for celebrities. She and I had never had more than the most limited of conversations, all of them having to do with work or food.

Most of the wait staff work their way up. First they buss tables, then they wait lunch, and, if they've proved themselves worthy, they finally get the dinner covers where the big money is to be made. With her looks, to-the-manor-born air, and almost mechanical efficiency, she immediately snapped up the most coveted nights of the week, Tuesday (opera night), Thursday (symphony night), and Friday and Saturday. Like most of the younger staff, she claims to be an actress. She's had some modeling gigs and a few bit parts in commercials. I can't image her actually acting, but she'd be a natural for those bitchy sorts of roles perfected by Joan Collins.

While waiting for her to come back with my water, I marveled at the difference between Drew and me. If someone had knocked on my door at ten at night, most likely I'd be in the Villains of Disneyland nightshirt my sister got me for my birthday last year—one size fits all—with a pair of white athletic socks to keep my feet warm. And it wouldn't be clouds of *Joy* you'd smell. More like the chalky, mint scent of Colgate with Tartar Control. To make myself really feel bad I started comparing the no doubt priceless carpet leading up to her apartment with the imitation oriental runner I'd picked up at Cost Plus for my own hallway when it hit me. The get-up. The perfume. She had a date. Brent. The thought of Brent stiff and very dead in a coroner's icebox made me crave that water. With a fifth of Jack Daniel's as a chaser. Then I heard the flap-flap of her mules on the landing above the staircase, so I began rubbing my foot again.

As she descended the staircase, she carried a Baccarat tumbler filled with ice water.

"Here you are," she said, handing me the glass with so little grace that the water almost slopped over the top. "How's your foot? I hope I didn't hurt you."

"Oh, it'll be fine in a couple of minutes," I assured her and took very tiny sips of my water. Surely she wouldn't throw me out until I'd finished my water. Her head had a distinct tilt to it, like she was listening for footsteps.

"Drew, Teri was at the funeral," I lied.

Her perfectly sculpted eyebrows arched in automatic disdain. She didn't see Teri as a threat. I was going to have to stick the knife in a little more.

"She told me something interesting," I continued. "Brent's got some sort of scam going on at the restaurant." I twisted the knife. "I was sure if she knew, you'd know."

"Why don't you ask Brent?" Her voice was so cold I practically saw her breath.

"Well, I didn't have a chance to talk with him," which was true in a creepy way. "I'm afraid if the police question Teri, she'll say something. I hoped you'd be able to fill me in. You know, with my ex being a cop, I've got lots of contacts in S.F.P.D. If it was something minor, I might be able to fix it."

Drew's porcelain perfect skin mottled into a sickly orange; she practically spat at me. "No, I don't know anything about it."

I began to believe her. She of the size five pants and size five feet had been left in the dust by someone with hair the color of carrots, size nine feet, and size fourteen pants. Drew was the girlfriend to show off to other people, a trophy on his arm, a walking vision in Armani. Teri was the one who listened to his fears and hopes.

But I needed to be sure. I pressed further. "Are you sure he didn't say something about padding the invoices or anything like that?"

"No, goddammit. He didn't tell me a thing," she snapped, past being polite. To regain her equilibrium she starting taking stock. Her hands cupped the seventy-five-dollar haircut behind her ears. She checked to see if her pearl earrings were intact and gave her manicured nails a glance. Perfect, no chips, I almost heard her say to herself.

Having ascertained that all was right in the world, she looked up and seemed startled to see me still there. Her eyes narrowed into menacing slits.

"I see you've finished your water. Good night." Walking over to me, she grabbed the nearly full glass out of my hand, splashing water all over the floor in the process. She ignored the mess and opened the door for me to exit.

I left without comment. She locked the door behind me and turned off the porch light. I guess she assumed Brent wasn't coming, or she was going to punish him by making him stand in that dark entryway until she felt like opening the door to him.

Teri Baxter wouldn't make him wait endlessly at the bottom of a long staircase. She'd be standing near the door, waiting for his footfall, not even giving him a chance to ring the doorbell before she opened it with arms flung wide. His excuses about being late wouldn't faze her, she'd be grateful to him for just showing up. I know which one I'd want to come home to.

I walked slowly down Chestnut, past the chic restaurants that spelled out the demise of the old neighborhood, hit Lombard, and made my way back to the motel. The fog was beginning to spread its wispy fingers over Cow Hollow. Once inside my room, I threw my purse on the chair, washed out my underwear, undressed, and got into bed. As I went to turn off the table lamp, my hand knocked the receiver off the telephone. The dial tone screeched at me to make my call.

I remembered what I'd forgotten, what had nagged me when I left the police station. I'd forgotten to call O'Connor. The shit was going to hit the fan.

Chapter 15

I fished in my purse for O'Connor's beeper number. He picked it up so fast it didn't even ring. I let him yell for about five minutes without me saying anything. Despite feeling incredibly guilty, I was getting a vicarious thrill that someone was actually worried about me. Apart from my mother and Amos, no one cares about my comings and goings these days.

After a while he stopped for air and I butted in. "O'Connor, I'm really sorry, but I completely forgot about calling you. After my session downtown I was so tired I didn't trust myself to drive across the bridge. I got in my car and drove to the first motel I found with a vacancy sign. I'm so sorry."

"Where are you?" he demanded.

"The Seadrift Inn on Lombard. I'm fine. I chowed down a big dinner, just had a long hot shower, and now I'm ready to go to sleep. I'll come out to your place in the morning and we can compare notes."

"Get your ass in your car right now and come on over to my house," he ordered. "Someone could have followed you from the station. You could be in danger. We'll make up a bed for you."

Now that the fog had come in it was cold in my room. I bunched the covers around my neck. There was no way in hell I was going to get into wet underwear and drive out to the Richmond.

"O'Connor, come on. No one followed me. Everything's okay. I'll call you first thing when I wake up."

"Look, Mary." His voice was stern. "This isn't an option on your part. As the detective on this case, I'm officially ordering you to leave that motel room right now."

I just sort of heard the last part, as if one of my ears worked and the other one didn't, because I saw the thin edge of a credit card trying to ease open the spring on my door. The person on the other side felt the mechanism slide back and began pushing the door open.

I dropped the phone, ran to the chair, and grabbed it, the contents of my purse spilling onto the cheap carpet. I wedged the chair under the door, holding it with my weight. I started screaming as loud and as long as I could. My assailant had wedged the door open a crack, but the chair held firm. I was strong—years of hauling around sixty-eight-pound blocks of butter build muscles—but I didn't know how long I could keep this up. I kept screaming and screaming, but the tug of war continued. Jesus Christ, wasn't anybody out there listening? I pushed the chair with every ounce of strength I possessed and the door closed.

I ran to the phone. No dial tone. Shit! As I frantically banged the buttons on the top of the cradle, I saw the credit card easing its way up the doorjamb again. Spying my Swiss Army knife on the floor, I lunged for it, fumbled with the sheath, and unfolded whatever blade came out first. I hacked at the card, trying to slice off the end so it wouldn't be long enough to release the spring. Suddenly, the card disappeared. I collapsed against the wall near the door, crumpling down into an exhausted heap.

From the other side of the door voices began yelling at each other in Spanish, with lots of grunting and groaning, like a fight was going on. Police sirens began wailing in the distance. Next, I heard a high-pitched thin scream and then a mournful, "*Madre de Dios*," and a thud against the door, as if someone had fallen against it, and then nothing.

I waited. A moment later, I heard several people shouting and then a bullhorn called my name. I looked up and saw a blue-red police light play on the walls and ceiling of the room. It took a while to get up, every muscle ached. I opened the door. The parking lot was filled with an ambulance, six police cars, and about ten police officers with their guns drawn. Nobody moved or said a word. They just blinked. I didn't have any clothes on. Stumbling back into the room, I pulled the cheap throw off the bed, wrapped it around me, and reappeared to face yet another contingent of the S.F.P.D.

A couple of female cops came up to me and escorted me to a police car. I climbed in and huddled against the leather, cocooning myself in the bedspread. One of them asked if I wanted anything. I shook my head no. I blanked out for a few minutes until O'Connor showed up. Considering he lived in the Richmond and this was Cow Hollow, he didn't do too badly.

When I'd dropped the phone to grab the chair, O'Connor heard me screaming on the other end. Why I couldn't get a dial tone was because he was still on the line. When I dropped the phone the second time, he used his cell phone to issue a call for every police car in a two-mile radius to storm the motel. I was pretty much alone in my end of the motel. The patrons who did hear me scream thought it was a domestic spat and didn't want to get involved.

"Eat something, then we'll talk," he ordered.

I was too tired to object. He brought me a greasy, hot, hamburger, swimming in mayonnaise, and a huge glass of milk from the coffee shop. I sat in the back of the police car and arranged the throw around me so I could eat. O'Connor stood next to the door, periodically checking to see how I was doing. All this was done in monosyllables like "eat" and "eat more." Once I had finished the hamburger I felt a lot better. The food blunted the shock. I handed him the empty plate.

"I need to get dressed. I'm freezing in this thing."

"In a minute." He glanced in the direction of the ambulance. His voice was clipped and cold. What bug crawled up his butt?

I looked over to where the ambulance was parked, its lights flashing furiously. A bunch of technicians were bent over a body, strapping whoever it was onto a gurney. They hoisted the guy up into the cab of the ambulance and sped away, sirens blaring.

"Who's in the ambulance? A cop get hurt trying to nab that pervert?" I hitched the bedspread around me even tighter. The fog was thick by now, enveloping the motel in its cold gray blanket.

O'Connor didn't look at me. "It's Gilberto Perez."

My arms went slack. I felt the bedspread snake its way down my torso.

"No way, O'Connor. No fucking way would he try to hurt me."

"Cool your jets, Ryan. He wasn't trying to hurt you. He tried to save you. We'll have to wait to get his side of the story, but one of the residents poked his head out the door to see what you were screaming about. He saw Perez attack the guy trying to jimmy open your door. The other guy knifed him."

"Is he going to make it?" I asked solemnly.

"It doesn't look good, but he's got a chance. When I called that code blue an ambulance was automatically sent to the scene. We got to him right away."

The hamburger that had warmed my bones not five minutes ago was tearing my stomach lining to shreds. I leaned my head against the back seat of the police car and closed my eyes.

"Snap out of it, Mary. Get dressed. You've been holding out on me. I'm so mad at you I could wring your scrawny neck."

I didn't open my eyes, but continued to sit there, waiting for my stomach to settle. "You snap out of it, O'Connor. I did hold out on you and the only person it hurt was that poor kid. If he dies, I won't be able to live with myself. I'll tell you the whole story in the morning. Are you still offering me a bed?"

No response.

I opened my eyes. O'Connor sat on the other side of the bench seat. His hands clutched his knees with such fury that his knuckles gleamed white against the dark interior of the car.

I covered his hand with my thin one and squeezed hard.

"Gilberto didn't do it on his own. You saved my life, too. Thanks."

He slid away from my hand. As he scooted out the door he ordered, "Get dressed, Mary. Moira's expecting us."

A policewoman appeared with my clothes in hand, escorted me to another motel room (mine was being dusted for prints), and waited for me while I got dressed. I balled up my wet underwear and shoved it in my purse.

O'Connor arranged for someone to drive my car while I sat in the front seat with him. We didn't speak one word to each other the entire drive. O'Connor's wife, Moira, sat at the kitchen table waiting for us, clutching a cup of tea. Her knuckles were white, her shoulders hunched, yet her body had a settled curve to it; she was in a familiar pose—like praying. When we came through the back door, I actually saw the tension in her body ratchet down several notches.

Moira was nice, if limited. She delivered nine months to the day from her wedding night and had stayed home with her children. We had almost nothing in common, but muddled through our social encounters with as much grace as possible and over the years had come to a satisfactory relationship. She bragged about her kids and the Boy Scouts, and I regaled her with food-industry gossip.

"How are you doing, Mary?" she asked, a tired, tentative smile on her face. The last two years hadn't been kind to her. Her hair, dyed a harsh yellow, made her look much older than she was. Or maybe it was the frown lines now firmly etched in her face. Of course, who was I to talk? I'd just spent two hundred dollars on a makeover that afternoon and then promptly washed it down my kitchen sink. My face still itched from the dish soap.

O'Connor cut me off before I could reply. "Moira, please show Mary to her room. We'll talk in the morning."

Moira outfitted me with a nightgown, extra toothbrush, and towels (she was the kind of woman who has that sort of thing "on hand"). Giving me a quick hug, she whispered, "Sleep well," and quietly closed the door. She'd rustled their eleven-year-old out of his room to bunk with one of his brothers.

I slept like the dead and didn't wake up until ten. I felt disoriented for a few minutes until I sorted out why I woke up in a room where the walls were virtually papered with posters of the Forty-Niner quarterback Steve Young. The house was quiet; the kids had already left for school. I lumbered out of the bedroom into the kitchen and stood squinting just inside the doorway.

It was sunny in the Richmond. In October, you have one month of beautiful sunrises, which in no way, shape, or form compensate for the damp, gray, suicide-promoting mornings the rest of the year. O'Connor's kitchen faces east and the whole room was brilliant with sunlight. I closed my eyes and let the hot light warm my bones. O'Connor's voice broke through my reverie.

"Working on your tan?" he asked sarcastically. He'd been sitting at the kitchen table, waiting for me to wake up. The newspaper looked like it had been mauled by wild animals. From the tone of his voice it was obvious he was still furious with me.

I beat my chest three times. "Mea culpa for Christ's sake."

I sat down in a chair, faced the sun, and closed my eyes. "Stop being angry with me, O'Connor, or we're not going to get anywhere. You know I can match you nasty remark for nasty remark. I suggest we carry on with our shaky truce."

Silence for a couple of minutes, then, "You want some coffee, a latte, espresso?" I opened half an eye. He held up a white dishtowel and waved it like a flag. "Cease fire?"

"Cease fire accepted. A latte, heavy on the milk," I yawned. An espresso would have fit the bill perfectly, but I wasn't sure how together my stomach was going to be after last night. While listening to the comforting sounds of milk being steamed, I looked around.

"This is great," I said, sweeping the room with my hand. They'd remodeled the kitchen since the last time I'd been there. Stainless steel countertops, industrial stove, terra-cotta tile floor, even a stainless steel-fronted refrigerator. Not the sort of kitchen Moira would have wanted. She'd have had the French Provincial tiles, bleached oak cabinets, the Sub-Zero fridge with front that matched the cabinets, Mexican pavers on the floor, and lace at the windows.

O'Connor put a latte in front of me. "How did you convince Moira to let you do this?"

"You know us. I screamed for ten minutes. Moira pouted for three weeks. Finally, I made a deal with her. I pointed out that since the rest of the house had become a living shrine to Martha Stewart, I had the right to do the kitchen my way. I do ninety percent of the cooking anyway. She could redo our bedroom, but the kitchen was mine. You wouldn't believe what she spent in linens and curtains. Jesus Christ, the paint alone was fifty dollars a gallon."

"It was precisely $45.39 a gallon. Pennies compared to that refrigerator you bought." Moira came into the kitchen, her handbag slung over her shoulder. She paused in front of the door to the garage.

"Got to run, Mary. Hope you got some sleep. Sorry we didn't get to talk." She turned to O'Connor. "I've got a PTA meeting at the school."

"I figured."

"Johnny's game is tonight. You going to make it?"

O'Connor jaw tightened. "I'm on a case, Moira."

"I figured." She walked out the door.

Embarrassed, I picked up the paper and pretended to read the front page. Funny, when you're married these skirmishes don't seem that serious, but to an onlooker, the alarm is ringing loud and clear.

"I called the hospital."

I put down the paper.

"Perez is holding his own. He's still in intensive care, but the doc thinks he can be moved to the floors later on today. She'll know better after lunch."

A tremendous weight lifted off my shoulders. I didn't want that one on my conscience. "Thanks, O'Connor. I appreciate it."

"You want a shower before you tell me what happened? And I mean everything," he emphasized.

I thought for a moment and decided not. I smelled a little yeasty, but I wanted to finish my latte before the milk got cold. "Nah."

"I want the dope on Perez first. Don't leave anything out."

I told him about seeing Gilberto in the paint store parking lot, the phone call, and our final encounter at Rosa's house.

"Look, I know what you're going to say. All this sounds suspicious, but he didn't murder anybody. I'd stake my life on it."

O'Connor picked up the white dishtowel and slapped the table, hard.

"It might come down to that. Mary, I can't believe you were a cop's wife. How do you know he didn't have anything to do with Brent's death?"

"Before you have a stroke, listen to me. Gilberto wasn't afraid or remorseful. He sounded frustrated and angry. He and Rosa had a big fight while I was there. She asked me to snoop around and Gilberto went ballistic, warning me to stay away from the restaurant. Not what I'd call killer mentality."

"Christ, Mary, you're driving me nuts." He balled up the towel and pitched it across the room. "You're too smart to be this naïve. If his brother was involved in this scam, what makes you think Perez isn't part of it too? He might have warned you away from the restaurant precisely because he's mixed up in it. Doesn't want you snooping around. Just because he tried to save your life doesn't mean he's not involved as well. Would you let me do my job?"

"I just…" I began protesting, then shut up. If I had called O'Connor and told him Gilberto was at Rosa's, they would have picked him up and he wouldn't be fighting for his life right now at S.F. General. Of course, I'd probably be dead meat by now, but I didn't want to dwell on that.

I held up my hand like the good Girl Scout I used to be. "No more secrets, I promise."

"Now tell me what happened from the moment you left the station until the cruisers got to your motel room."

"As I said on the phone, I completely spaced out touching bases with you after I made my statement. I drove down Lombard and stopped at the first motel with a vacancy sign. I checked in, showered, ate, and realized I was about three blocks from Drew's place. I walked over there, talked to her, and left. When I got back I realized I hadn't called you, and well, you know the rest."

"This the rich girlfriend? I questioned her a couple of days ago. Very cool customer. She claims Brent wasn't at her house the night of Carlos' murder. Said she and Vamos were together at her house until around three, finalizing the schedule for the charity gig. Coroner says Perez was killed about two in the morning, although he's willing to stretch it an hour either way if I press him. That lets them off the hook for now."

I was a little surprised. I never saw Drew and Juan particularly chummy.

"Christ, this case is just a series of dead ends." O'Connor sighed and rubbed his neck. "Just curious, but what's she doing working in the restaurant? From her address and the furniture in her place, I bet she could buy American Fare and not even have it make a dent in her bank account."

"You're right, she comes from money, but she likes the restaurant scene. She has to do something with her time. Plus she's a celebrity junkie. She waited on Robert Redford last week and nearly raised an eyebrow she was so excited."

"Did you tell her about Brent?"

"No, she didn't know. She was all dolled up in a six-hundred-dollar pair of lounging pajamas, obviously waiting for Brent. The perfume was laid on pretty thick. It was kind of creepy knowing she was going to be stood up. I asked her if Brent had told her anything about the scam he was running. She got really pissed off at me because she was out of the loop, for once. She basically threw me out of her house."

"I gotta talk to her. She knows about Brent by now, it's all over the media. Bigger than when Masa got his. You should demand hazard pay the way chefs are getting bumped off in this city. I'll ask her if she saw anything when you left. I'll bring up the scam and get my own take on it."

"I seriously doubt whether she saw anyone follow me. She slammed the door behind me so hard it felt like an aftershock from the Loma Prieta earthquake."

"Well, I need to question her again. You know, Mary, maybe it's not a scam. Maybe Brent's been blackmailing her. She's the only person in this picture who has big money."

I couldn't picture Drew, the ice queen, capitulating to a blackmailer's demands.

"Mmm, that's pretty far-fetched. Besides, you never saw them together. Brent was always terrified he wasn't cool enough for her. He was like a nervous puppy around her. I half expected him to pee on her shoes every now and then. That doesn't fit with him blackmailing her. Besides, with her money she could hire an assassin to get rid of some petty blackmailer."

O'Connor stood up and shoved his chair under the table. "Maybe that's exactly what she did. Chung's subpoenaing their bank records to make sure. It's either sex or money. I'll go to her place after I talk to Perez. He's my only lead right now. After I talk to that Summers woman, I'll meet you at your mother's house and we'll brainstorm this afternoon. I want to know how the restaurant works, the laundry delivery system, produce, meat, and dairy deliveries, the wine shipments, how you decide which wine to order, that sort of thing."

He crunched his neck to one side. "My neck is killing me. Must have slept wrong. Moira's left you a pair of sweats in the bathroom you can borrow. You jump in the shower and call me the minute you get to your mother's. Here's the number again." He handed me yet another business card. "In fact, I want to talk to your mother to make sure you're actually there."

"Oh, come on," I protested. "What are we? Ten years old?"

O'Connor put both hands on the kitchen table and leaned toward me. His face was four inches away from mine. I smelled coffee and milk on his breath. My spine began tingling; the current ran down my legs and left my toes numb.

"Look, Ryan. What makes you think that what happened to Brent couldn't happen to you? Your track record stinks. You almost got killed last night. Do you want your mother to read about your bloody body being found in some no-name motel on Lombard?"

I wrapped my arms around myself and looked away from his face.

"Of course not."

"And by the way, I called your mother early this morning to let her know where you were so she wouldn't see the papers and go crazy with worry."

Gallons of guilt washed over me. Someone gets killed in your bed, you should tell your mother right away.

He pointed a menacing finger at me.

"You have an hour and a half to get to your mother's house. That'll give you plenty of time to take a quick shower and drive across the bridge. If I haven't heard from you by noon," this was accompanied by more vigorous finger-pointing, "I'm going to put out an APB on you."

He cleared our coffee cups from the table and started to leave out the side door to the garage.

"Hey," I called, and he turned around to face me.

"What now?"

"My mom, thanks for calling her," I said to the table.

"No problem. Before you take your shower, check out our bedroom. You can't even find the bed for all the frou-frou shit everywhere. Every morning when I wake up, I thank the Virgin Mary I haven't choked to death on my pillow." Then he left.

I should've had an espresso I still felt groggy, like I had mashed potatoes for brains. Searching through the cupboards, I found some sort of flakes reportedly healthy for your innards, but lathered with sugar to make it palatable to kids. All that sugar made me feel a hell of a lot better.

Chapter 16

I showered, dressed, and made good time across the bridge. So good, in fact, I decided to peek in on Teri Baxter. She lives pretty close to my mom. I'd check and see if she had contacted the police yet. What harm could five minutes do?

There were plenty of parking spaces in the lot in front of her apartment. Getting out of my car, I heard someone's stereo cranked up to the max. As I got closer, I realized it was her stereo and her door was slightly ajar.

I knocked and yelled her name. No answer. I knocked again, louder this time, yelled her name, still no answer. I wasn't surprised. The windows were practically shaking in their frames, the music was so loud. I gingerly pushed the door forward and inched my head around the doorframe.

Shards of broken glass and dishes littered the cheap carpet. All of her gay Italian ceramics and Venetian goblets were smashed to bits. Giant gouges pockmarked the walls from the impact of the plates and glasses.

I stood there in shock for God knows how long, just panning around the room at the total destruction. The sixth time around, I noticed the bathroom door was shut tight. I tiptoed through the mess, turned off the stereo, and tried the door. Locked. I thought I could hear faint whimpering.

"Teri, are you in there? It's Mary, Mary Ryan from the restaurant," I yelled through the door.

Immediately, Teri started sobbing hysterically "Have they gone? Are they still there?"

"Teri, it's all right. I'm here. No one's here but me. Come out now."

I heard her fumble with the knob, but she was so shaky she couldn't get the door open.

"Listen to me, wash your face and sit down for a few minutes to get your breath. When you've calmed down, try the door again."

More hysterics for a while, then the sobbing gradually subsided. Like a mantra, I kept saying through the door, everything is okay, I'm here, calm down. Finally she stopped crying and I heard her turn on the taps.

While she was washing up, I got a garbage bag from the kitchen. The glass had shattered into millions of tiny pieces, but that Italian ceramic is strong stuff and broke into large chunks I could pick up with my hands.

I'd picked up about half of it when the door opened. She stood in the doorframe, still afraid to come into the room. As her eyes catalogued the complete destruction of all her lovely glasses and plates, she started crying again, that silent, you-don't-even-know-the-tears-are-streaming-down-your face kind of grief. I dropped the garbage bag.

I grabbed Teri by the shoulders and tried to make eye contact with her.

"Teri, look at me."

She shrank away from my voice and tucked her head into the crook of my shoulder.

"We need to leave. Okay?" I wrapped my arms around her and stroked her head for a couple of minutes. Then I stepped back, cupped her chin, and with the gentlest of gestures brought her face-to-face with me. "Okay?" I repeated. Finally, her eyes met mine and there was the barest nod of the head.

"We're getting out of here. My mother lives close by; she's a nurse. She'll check you out to make sure you're all right."

Teri looked at me blankly. I wasn't sure if she'd heard me or not.

"Teri, where's your purse?" I demanded.

Her eyes sort of flickered toward the television. I grabbed her purse and slung it over my arm.

"We're leaving now," I said firmly. Still no response. I took that as a yes. I put my arm around her and hustled her out of the apartment and into my car. She was on autopilot. I buckled her seat belt for her.

"Teri, I'm going to lock up your apartment. I'll be back in five seconds." Her hand halfheartedly rose up to stop me from leaving her.

I ran back to her place and tried to lock the door. The lock was damaged. I pulled the door shut, hoping she had renter's insurance. Hightailing it back to the car, I ran every stop sign between Teri's apartment and my mother's house. I made it in a record three minutes.

Once my stepfather ascertained we were alive with no broken bones, he retreated to the back room and the radio set and my mom took over.

My mom is the greatest. She took one look at Teri and immediately smothered her with hugs and smiles, no questions asked. Ten minutes later, a mug of hot, sweet tea had restored Teri to the human world. She still wasn't talking, but her eyes had lost that dead look. I made my phone call to O'Connor.

He sounded relieved, unaware there had been a little change in the program.

"So, Ryan, you made it to your mother's house in one piece. I was just about to call and read you the riot act again for not calling me. Did you get a look at all the lace and stenciling crap…"

"Look, O'Connor," I interrupted. "I happened to pass by Teri Baxter's place on my way to my mom's and thought I'd check up on her. When I got there her door was open, and her apartment was trashed. She'd locked herself in the bathroom. I still haven't gotten a word out of her, but she's all right."

The professional in him took over. Curt and brusque, he started asking questions that sounded like orders. Are you currently at your mother's house? What's Teri Baxter's address? Did you see anyone in or around the apartment? At what time did you arrive at Ms. Baxter's apartment? Did Ms. Baxter sustain any injuries? Have you sustained any injuries? Once he had ascertained that neither Teri nor I was hurt, he told me to sit tight.

"I'm calling the Kensington police and asking them to station two men at your mother's house. Wait for me. Keep your butts inside. Don't open the door to anyone except the cops. No one. Don't even call anyone. Is that clear?" He didn't bother to get my answer. "I'm going over to Ms. Baxter's place right now. I'll be up to question her once the forensics crew gets there." He hung up.

True to O'Connor's word, five minutes later, a squad car from the local police department pulled into the driveway, with two very serious-looking cops in the front seat. We got a controlled wave, nothing else. My mom, Teri, and I went back to sit at the kitchen table, waiting for O'Connor.

My mother and I gossiped about the family, chitchatted about this and that, while the color returned to Teri's face. Teri didn't say anything; she just sat there with a big steaming mug of tea my mother buys directly from Ireland. It's so strong you can stand a fork in it. You have to put tons of sugar and milk in it to make it palatable, but once doctored up…aah. The acrid taste of the tea bounces off the sugar. Nectar.

O'Connor came by about an hour and a half later. Teri was in my old bedroom, fast asleep. Despite all the caffeine, she had asked to lie down for a few minutes and before we knew it, snores and snorts were coming from the bedroom.

My mother and O'Connor have a playful, flirtatious relationship. They liked each other on sight, Black Irish to Black Irish, and have met at various functions. It always irritates the shit out of me, this fun banter they toss back and forth. Whenever I made noises about what a political and social pig he was, my mother would laugh and say he and I weren't that far apart, we just liked to fight with each other. Today, thank God, they dispensed with their usual slightly bawdy humor.

Once he ascertained that Teri was peacefully asleep, he positioned himself at the kitchen table with the laptop and began to grill me about my movements since I left his house. After picking my brains for forty-five minutes, he asked my mother to wake up Teri. It was time to hear the first half of the story.

Shuffling into the kitchen like she was a hundred years old, Teri slowly eased herself into a chair. Sleep had done her few favors; her face was splotchy and swollen, and her hair hung in disheveled clumps like limp carrots. She'd slept in her clothes last night and the nap had piled new wrinkles on top of old ones. But when she finally came face to face with O'Connor she looked calm and when she spoke she was coherent.

It was clear from her demeanor that she didn't have a clue about Brent's death. "I've been avoiding the police 'cause I didn't want to answer any questions about Brent. I'm sorry, Inspector O'Connor." She looked up at O'Connor with the innocence of a five-year-old. "I wanted to talk with him and let him know that I had screwed up, you know, talked to Mary about what he'd told me. I bet he's going to be real mad at me," she said wistfully.

Now that she had gotten started, she couldn't stop.

"I didn't even go to Carlos' funeral, which made me sad 'cause I really liked him, but I was afraid the police would be there and I hadn't been able to reach Brent. I even called him twice at home, which was so scary because I'm really afraid of his wife, but he wasn't there. I just stayed in my place watching movies with the headphones on, not making a peep. I was afraid to even flush the toilet. I wanted to talk to Brent before I talked to the police." She thrust her chin at O'Connor in a small show of defiance. "I just kept quiet. Until this morning."

"Tell me everything you can remember, Ms. Baxter. What your attackers looked like, the color of their hair, eyes, height, weight. Any little detail is important," O'Connor reminded her.

"It was about eight this morning. I'd fallen asleep watching videos and I was still in my clothes. I heard the buzzer, then someone yelled, 'Police, open up. We know you're in there.' I figured this time I was really going to have to talk to you guys. I went over to the door and looked out the peephole." She stopped talking and began biting her nails.

"What did you see?" prompted O'Connor.

"Two men with stockings over their faces," she whispered.

"Were they tall, short? Describe them to me."

"The peephole makes everyone look squat and far away. All I can tell you is that they were about the same size."

"What did you do?" O'Connor asked gently.

"When I didn't respond, they began forcing the door open." Teri started crying. "I…I ran into the kitchen, grabbed the biggest knife I have and locked myself in the bathroom just in time. I heard them enter the apartment. Then they turned up the stereo and starting smashing all my plates and glasses." She was sobbing now, her violent crying filling up the small breakfast nook.

O'Connor let her cry for a couple of minutes, then said to me quietly, "Get her some water."

I got up, gave her a big hug, filled up a tumbler with water, and handed it to her.

She drank it slowly. When she had finished it, she looked exhausted but calm.

"I'm okay, now, thanks." She gave me a tiny smile. "Once they had smashed all my stuff, they turned off the stereo for a second to scream at me some more and then they turned it back on and left. I was too terrified to leave the bathroom. I thought they might come back. I stayed in there until Mary arrived."

O'Connor adopted the tone he usually reserves for small children. "So, Ms. Baxter, what exactly did they say to you?"

"Well…." She was whispering again. We all leaned toward her to hear what she was saying. "They said not to say anything to the police or they would kill me next time."

We almost missed the last bit because her lips barely moved.

"Any other threats? What did they say exactly?" he probed.

She closed her eyes. "They told me, 'Keep your fucking mouth shut or you'll end up in a laundry bag, too' and 'If you don't shut the fuck up, your funeral will be next Monday.'"

O'Connor glanced down at his notes and frowned. "Okay, let's see. You can't tell me how tall they were. Did you recognize them?"

Teri opened her eyes, all iris from fear. My mother took hold of one of her hands, and Teri grasped tightly.

"No, the stockings mushed up their faces. Their hair was really black and their skin dark. You know, not black, but dark. When they were throwing all my plates against the wall, I heard those jerks laughing over the music," she said bitterly.

"Can you tell me anything about their voices? High, deep, did both of them talk or did only one of them threaten you?"

"Only one of them threatened me. He had a deep voice. It sounded, you know, familiar to me."

"Familiar?" O'Connor said sharply.

"Yeah, but maybe that's only because he sounded like someone from the restaurant."

I butted in, "What do you mean from the restaurant? Someone specific?"

"Yeah, maybe, I mean accent-wise, you know."

"Ms. Baxter." O'Connor wanted to be sure on this point. "Are you telling me that you recognized one of the men who made threats against you?"

"Well, sort of. I guess I mean they sounded like a lot of the guys I work with."

"Ms. Baxter, did you or did you not recognize the men who trashed your apartment."

O'Connor was getting impatient with her, I could tell from his voice.

"I don't k...k...know." She began to get weepy again. "They were Hispanic, okay? I just don't know. Why is everyone getting so worked up over a few bottles of wine?"

My mouth dropped open. I was certain she'd never even hinted that the scam involved wine.

"Teri," I demanded. "What wine?"

O'Connor kicked my shin. His subtle way of telling me to shut up.

Teri stopped crying and turned toward me. "You told me you knew. You lied to me," she accused. "I thought you were my friend."

For no reason, all of a sudden I felt horribly guilty. Like I was the one trying to manufacture alibis for my crooked boyfriend.

"Teri, I didn't actually lie to you. I...I let you think I knew more than I did."

My mother gave me a stern look, and O'Connor gave me another even bigger kick to keep quiet.

"Ms. Baxter, what do you remember Mr. Brown telling you about the wine?"

She didn't have anything to add to the story. It was verbatim what she had told me, but with the little bit about the scam centering on wine sales. Once he was satisfied that she was clueless on the nature of the wine scam, he began drilling her about the night of Carlos' murder. Was she with Chef Brown the night Carlos was killed? She didn't answer him for the longest time, just sat there staring down at the placemat in front of her.

He tried again. "Ms. Baxter, did you hear me? Did you see Chef Brown between the hours of midnight and six a.m., the night of Mr. Perez's murder?"

Still not making eye contact with any of us, she countered with, "Would that give Brent an alibi?"

My mother and I looked away toward the garden.

"Chef Brown doesn't need an alibi for the night of the murder, Ms. Baxter. Now, for form's sake, were you with him between the hours of midnight and six a.m. the night of Mr. Perez's murder?"

"Well, I didn't get off my shift until eleven-thirty. Brent was still there. I didn't see him after that," she conceded. "I guess that leaves me without an alibi, too. As if that matters," she sighed. "He was suppose to come over yesterday. We had a date, but I guess with the funeral and everything, he couldn't make it."

Brent couldn't make that date or any other date.

O'Connor gently led her through their conversation about the wine three or four more times, asking the same questions over and over again. She didn't know anything more than that one stupid drunken comment by Brent, which had nearly gotten her killed.

O'Connor had questioned Teri for about two hours when finally he decided he'd gotten all he was going to get out of her. He snapped his laptop shut.

"I guess that pretty much wraps it up, Ms. Baxter. You can't go back to your apartment just yet. Is there any place that you can stay in the meantime? Do you have family close by?"

She shook her head vigorously. "No, my parents live in Ohio."

My mother, bless her heart, chimed in, "She can stay here. We've got plenty of room."

Teri gave her a small smile and nodded. I gave my mother an exasperated look. That was all very nice but where was I going to stay? I wasn't going back to my place until it was cleaned up.

O'Connor gave my mother a grin of conspiratorial approval. "That's very nice of you, Mrs. Grant. In a couple of hours I'll send up a patrol car so Ms. Baxter can get some clothes. I'm sure she'll be very comfortable here. Ms. Baxter, do you think you could come down to headquarters tomorrow morning?"

She nodded and then O'Connor motioned my mother over to his side, whispered in her ear for a couple of minutes, and turned to hike a thumb in my direction. "You, in my car."

Chapter 17

O'Connor saluted the two cops on watch and opened his car's passenger door.

"In," he ordered.

Once we were both seated, he plugged his laptop into the cigarette lighter and began reading off the screen.

"First of all, you're cleared of Brent's murder."

"Murder," I repeated, not a question.

"Yeah, Brown's prints are the only ones on the gun, but the angle of the bullet doesn't work for suicide. Looks like the poor bastard was executed, the gun wiped clean, and then Brown's hand was manually placed on the grip. Pretty amateurish. Coroner did the prelim and says Brent was killed about two o'clock. The old man on your street says he saw Brent arrive at your place around one forty-five. Unfortunately, his meal wagon came just about then. He and the attendant began setting up his lunch, and he didn't see anyone else. None of the other neighbors were home. Chang checked with Nordstrom. At noon you got a massage, at one-thirty a makeover, at two—" O'Connor clicked and scrolled—"a hair cut, and at three you got your nails done. Airtight."

"Great." I breathed an internal sigh of relief. Not so good for Gilberto. I hoped Rosa could give him an alibi. "Is that it? I want to arrange to have my place cleaned up. Is the crime-scene tape gone?" I made a move to exit the car.

"Not so fast, I'm not done. Are you sure you were alone at the restaurant on Thursday morning?" He had a self-satisfied look, like a cat who'd had several pawfuls of cream.

"Yeah. If anyone else had been there, wouldn't they have been discovered when all the cops arrived? Why?"

"How well do you know Thom Woods?"

These questions weren't making any sense. Why drag Thom into this?

"He's worked at the restaurant for a couple of years. We don't get along too well, but that's just personal animosity on my part. Brent liked him, and even I've got to admit he's good at his job. What's going on?"

"A bum who sleeps in a doorway at the end of the alley was taking an early morning pee when he saw Woods coming out of the restaurant sometime after six. According to our records, you phoned in the murder at six twelve."

"Is this George you talked to? Bald on top, broken nose he never got set so it curves to the right, wears a dirty blue pea coat?"

"Yeah, that's him. You know the guy?"

"Not kissing cousins." Now there's a thought that made me immediately want to scour my mouth out with bleach. "Sometimes I give him leftover baked goods. The man's tanked most of the time. He's your witness?"

The homeless issue in San Francisco rages on with no winners. George is like hundreds of men, a Vietnam vet who came home to find himself an object of contempt. He needs to dry out and get some major psychiatric help, but the last time he tried the psychiatrist made him remember the war. The booze makes him forget.

O'Connor grimaced. "Not ideal, I agree. He recognized Woods. Twice last week Woods threatened to have him arrested when George got too close to his new car. Like most drunks he's a creature of habit. He sleeps in that doorway every night. When he wakes up he checks the Union 76 clock to see what time it is so he can go to St. Anthony's and get some grub."

"You mean the B of A clock," I reminded him. Bank of America recently put their imprint on the giant digital clock that stands sentinel over the Fremont Street off-ramp. I still do a double take every time I see it.

"Whatever. Any idea how Woods could have hidden in the restaurant without you knowing it? Walter's certain it was after six when he woke up. He's not sure about the exact time, all he looks for is the digital six. That's when St. Anthony's opens up."

I made a mental map of the restaurant, trying to envision where and how Thom might have hidden himself.

"He must have been upstairs. There's no place to hide downstairs unless he was in the walk-in, which I doubt. It's forty degrees in there."

"How many outside phone lines do you have?"

"Five." Bingo! "He was in the office!"

O'Connor smiled and nodded.

"When I phoned 911, he saw the light on the phone console and fled the restaurant. But why? He has a perfect right to be there."

O'Connor got a satisfied look on his face. "Not if he planned on hauling Perez's body out the door and dumping it in the water down at Pier 29. He saw the light flash on the phone, picked up the receiver, and heard you tell the dispatcher about Perez. He knew the game was up and ran out the door."

I found myself in the dubious position of leaping to Thom's defense.

"Thom the murderer? The guy gets faint every time he walks into the kitchen and we're filleting salmon. I'm not saying he's not capable of something illegal." I thought about his new car. "But murder?"

"When Chang did his preliminary investigation of the office on the day of the murder, he noticed the sophistication of the hardware, especially the printer. Chang's got a computer expert checking it out right now."

I remembered Thom's sweaty face the day after the murder and his insistent questions about the cops touching his computer. "Have you talked to him yet?"

"I was on my way to his place when you phoned me about the break-in at Teri Baxter's studio. Woods is in the perfect position." O'Connor began ticking off points with his fingers. "He has keys, comes and goes when he pleases, drives a new car, lives in Gramercy Towers...."

"No way," I protested. How in the hell could Thom afford to live on Nob Hill?

"Yep," said O'Connor smugly. "Moved in there six months ago. Still think he's innocent?"

All the petty arguments Thom and I have had over the last two years flashed in my mind. His posturing, his ass-kissing, his impossible demands. But there was also the day the prep cook was chopping the wings off chickens to make stock. Thom walked by just as the cleaver went whack, severing the wing from the carcass. Thom ran from the kitchen in horror, and we heard him retching in the bathroom.

"He didn't do it, O'Connor. I saw Carlos' face. It was beaten to a pulp. Thom might be snide, bitchy, and petty, but he's not violent. He routinely cups spiders in his hands and walks all the way from the office to the front door to let them free."

O'Connor slammed down the lid of his laptop. "But he verbally terrorizes feeble drunks just because they're pissing twenty feet from his car."

"That's exactly what I mean. You're not listening. As usual. He might pitch a hissy fit at Walter or Carlos, but he'd never hit anyone."

Any good will generated between us by the last three days' events evaporated.

He put the laptop in the back of the car, put the key in the ignition, and turned to me. His lips were taut, his voice sarcastic.

"Speaking of listening, I told you to go straight to your mother's house. What part of that sentence didn't you understand?"

I felt anger rush through my body, simmering at my toes and sizzling out the top of the head. I started to pant, I was so mad.

"You can't stand it when someone has the gall to challenge you. I say where I go and what I do. If I hadn't stopped by Teri's house, she'd still be cowering and whimpering in her bathroom. Or worse. They might have come back and finished her off. Take this investigation and shove it up your ass, O'Connor. You swagger around, silencing everyone in your wake with your overbearing, arrogant attitude. It doesn't work with me."

"Overbearing, arrogant?" he laughed. It was not a nice laugh. "You should know, sweetheart, you wrote the book. How Jim put up with your castra...."

Completely out of control, I raised my hand to smack his mouth, to stop him from finishing his sentence.

He was too fast for me. He cinched his fingers around my wrist like a vise. I tried to pull my arm free, he held fast.

Just as I was about to wrest my arm away from him in a final defiant gesture, our rage boiled over and metamorphosed into a mutual sexual longing so intense it threatened to melt the tires. I hadn't felt a lust this raw since I was eighteen. We stared at each other, transfixed with desire. Our hot, labored breath steamed up the car windows in five seconds flat.

As O'Connor's hand released my wrist with a slow caress, his thumb languidly stroked the inside of my palm. My cheeks flamed from desire and an involuntary moan escaped my lips. He brought his hand up again, cupped the back of my neck, and drew me to him. And, just like when I was eighteen, a medley of no-I-mustn'ts and yes-I-musts sang in my head. Six inches away, five inches away, the yes-I-musts were winning hands down, I couldn't stop myself. It had been so long...

O'Connor's cell phone rang. The high-pitched ring shattered the mood and restored sanity. O'Connor whipped his hand from my neck as if I had bubonic plague. As he fumbled to flip open his phone, I bolted from the car, tears of shame and frustration streaming down my cheeks.

Chapter 18

"Mary?" my mother's voice followed me down the hall as I raced past her to the bathroom. She and Teri were sitting in the living room.

"Be out in a minute."

I locked the door and sat on the toilet. This is a small house and any crying I did needed to be silent. I grabbed a bath towel and shoved my face into it, hoping it would completely muffle my sobbing.

How could I even think of kissing him? Not to mention the more involved sexual acrobatics I'd had in mind. I was the lowest of the low. I remembered that tense exchange in the kitchen between O'Connor and Moira, the brassy hair, the frown lines around her mouth and eyes, unhappiness written large on her face. I wasn't responsible for the state of the O'Connors' marriage, but I felt like I'd administered the *coup de grâce* to a wounded animal.

All that roasting of pigs, baking of pies, and tasting of wines was really a covert sexual dance between the two of us that we carried on without jeopardizing our marriages. And the arguing. Another way of sublimating the sexual energy between us. What were the lyrics to that Chrissy Hinds song? "There's a thin line between love and hate." I prayed that this revelation was as new to him as it was to me. I recalled that scene the day before yesterday in my kitchen, popping those cherry tomatoes in his mouth. I sat on the toilet, writhing with embarrassment.

I don't know how long I sat in there, berating myself over and over again.

A small knock, then, "Mary, are you all right?" came from the other side of the door.

I squeaked out a tremulous, "Fine, I need to wash my face."

I turned on the taps and splashed cold water over my inflamed cheeks, burning from desire or the crying jag, I didn't know which. Fortunately, I'd left my purse in the kitchen. Tiptoeing out of the bathroom into the breakfast nook, I grabbed my sunglasses to camouflage my raw, red eyes, and went into the living room.

It looked like a Norman Rockwell painting, my mother and Teri sitting side by side on the couch, Mom teaching Teri how to knit. I knew from the concerned pucker on my mother's face and the embarrassed look on Teri's face that all my efforts to keep my crying to myself were wasted.

"I need to go home, Mom." I left it at that. I gathered from all that whispering O'Connor and my mother had been doing earlier that she'd been put in charge of telling Teri about Brent's murder. From the serene look on Teri's face, I gathered that Mom hadn't relayed the bad news yet.

My mother stopped mid-purl and said firmly, "You are not staying there until this case is solved. Sleep on our couch."

"Oh, no, Mrs. Grant," Teri protested. "I'll sleep on the couch."

"Nobody's sleeping on the couch. I just called Amos," I lied. "I'm shacking up with him for a few days. I'm going to stop by my place and pick up some clothes."

"Are you sure you're all right?" The unspoken part of that sentence said, "I know you were bawling in the bathroom, what's going on?"

I wanted to scream at the top of my lungs, NO! Like some sex-crazed adolescent, I almost screwed O'Connor right in front of your house and I feel as guilty as hell!

"Absolutely. I'll call in a couple of hours when I've gotten settled." I walked out the door, forestalling any further protests.

I nodded at the cops stationed in the driveway, hoping against hope that neither of them had looked in the rearview mirror and seen our sexcapades. I pasted a smile on my face and waved bye at my mother, who was watching me from the window, her face wrinkled with worry.

When I pulled into my driveway the crime-scene tape was still up. Damn it to hell, I had no clothes other than the clothes I borrowed from Moira, now soaked in sweat, and the linen suit I had worn to Carlos' funeral, which was crumpled up into a ball in the back seat of my car.

Making good on my lie to my mother, I headed for the next freeway on-ramp and flipped open my cell phone.

"Amos, it's Mary. Can I park my butt at your place for a couple of days?"

"Girl, what is going on with you? Are you some sort of dead body magnet or what?"

Normally Amos's wicked sense of humor compliments my own. Today, however, it seemed a tad inappropriate.

I started blubbering again.

Amos spent the next fifteen miles apologizing and tried to stop my hysterics so I wouldn't kill myself on the bridge. I pulled off at Fremont Street. The B of A clock loomed over my car as I tried to negotiate the curve, hold my cell phone, and blow my nose—all at the same time.

"Are you off the freeway, yet?" Like he was coaching a seven-year-old trying to land a 747 jet, Amos spoke slowly and succinctly, his southern drawl in abeyance.

"Y…e…s…ssss," I sobbed.

"Park and get yourself together. You've been doing way too much boo-hooing. After you've calmed down, you drive over to my place. Just whipped up a batch of vanilla ice cream. I got bananas and macadamia nuts, I'll make the caramel right now."

The thought of a gooey, sweet banana split dried up my tears like magic.

"Sounds great. I'm just a couple minutes away from the restaurant. I'll swing by—those Boscs that came in last week are terrific—and I'll pick up some chocolate, too." Chocolate, pears, and freshly made ice cream. That should sublimate a few sexual urges. "I'll be over in twenty minutes."

The restaurant was deserted. I grabbed a bowl, threw in a few hunks of chocolate and went to the walk-in to get the pears. Coming out I noticed the crime-scene tape missing from the laundry closet. Juan must have gotten clearance from the police. The closet was full of fresh laundry in anticipation of our reopening.

My eyes darted from the gleaming white jackets and crisply pressed checked pants to the laundry bags piled on the floor filled with clean towels. Clean clothes versus total terror. In slow motion, my mind went over once again pulling down the sides of the laundry bag and flinching in horror at the sight of Carlos' beaten face.

I'd rather have eaten rotten eggs than go in there, but I really wanted some clean clothes.

I went to the bar, grabbed a bottle of Remy V.S.O.P., and downed a couple of gigantic swigs. I ran into the laundry closet, and wedging my feet between the laundry bags, I lurched my way across the room. Not wanting to spend one more second than I needed to, I didn't bother to hunt for my size but snatched a jacket and pants from the far end of the closet where the bigger sizes were, and fled upstairs to the office to change.

Thom's computer equipment and file cabinets were gone. They'd even hauled away his desk. It was like the Bermuda Office Triangle had swallowed up all traces of his existence.

I called Amos's number and put him on the speakerphone so I could talk and change clothes at the same time.

"It's me. I'm still at the restaurant. All Thom's equipment is gone, computer, file cabinets, even his desk. O'Connor told me he's their number one suspect."

I peeled off the sweats. The pants smelled like stale sex, all my pheromones riled up and no place to go.

Memo to self: wash sweats in scalding water, twice, before returning to Moira.

Amos snorted in disbelief. "They must be mighty desperate to think Thom had anything to do with either of those murders, especially Brent's. Brent was his bread and butter. Carlos? I don't think I saw Thom say two words to Carlos the entire two years he worked here."

Both the pants and jacket were way too big. The jacket I could live with. The pants? I grabbed a stapler from Juan's desk and stapled the waistband in a couple of places so they'd stay on my hips.

"That's what I told O'Connor. He told me Thom's bought a new car and moved to Nob Hill, all in the space of six months. Where's he getting all this money? He's paid well, but not that well."

"Not from his family, that's for sure. You asked me a couple of days ago why I don't come down on Thom. He and I are cut from the same cloth. His father's a Hasidic rabbi back in New York. Just like my papa, he disowned Thom's gay ass. His name used to be Wodinsky. His father made him change it, said he was a disgrace to his race and his religion. Felt like old home week when Thom told me that."

"He also has a jerky father, so what? That doesn't explain the car or the apartment," I reminded him. "Maybe Thom was embezzling. Brent found out so Thom killed him."

"Didn't happen, baby."

"What do you mean?" I picked up the receiver and turned off the speakerphone. Amos' voice lost that long-ago-far-away quality and became crystal clear.

"Thom was with me all day Monday."

I couldn't be hearing this right. "What do you mean, with you?"

"How graphic do you want it?"

I sat down on the edge of the nearest desk and tried to digest what Amos was telling me. On the one hand I felt vindicated. Eat rocks, O'Connor. On the other, here's my best friend telling me he's having some sort of relationship with a man whose character I assassinate on a daily basis.

"Amos, I'm having a hard time with this one."

"Yeah, I thought you might. Give me O'Connor's pager number. I gotta save Thom's hide. You still coming over?"

"In a little while. I've got some errands to run. I don't have any clothes, my house is still wrapped up in crime-scene tape."

"We've been friends too long to let this shit interfere. You going to be here sometime soon?"

"I promise. First, I need to go to Mervyn's and pick up some underwear," I lied.

If Thom didn't kill Brent, and, by default, Carlos, then who did? I needed to talk to Sharon and find out what was behind their office visit. The determination and vitriol in Sharon's voice when she insisted on removing anything incriminating from the office was proof enough for me that she had some knowledge about the financial shenanigans going on, who was cooking the books—and why. I might get some answers if I made noise about her being accessory after the fact, but then placate her by claiming I'd use my influence with S.F.P.D. on her behalf if she told me everything.

Before I left for Sharon's I went down to the kitchen and swiped a steak knife from the cutlery station. Using some first aid tape, I lashed it to my forearm and rolled my sleeve down to cover it. Just in case. I couldn't imagine Sharon hurting me, but the last few days had shown me that things were seldom what they seemed. I closed up the restaurant and drove to St. Francis Woods. Halfway there I realized I'd left the pears and chocolate back at the restaurant. Damn.

Chapter 19

All the way to St. Francis Woods, I went over everything I knew about the wine setup: how we added wines to the cellar, the delivery schedule, and the cellar itself. We choose wines based on staff tastings and recommendations. Once every couple of months, Brent, Juan, me, the sous chefs, and the top waiters sit around a table, taste a wine by itself, and then try it paired with food. Needless to say, on wine-tasting days, a jolly time is had by all. By the time I get to the dessert wines, I certainly am not feeling any pain.

The delivery is standard. Tuesdays and Thursdays for the liquor distributors. I often sign for the deliveries because most foodstuffs come early in the morning. We start baking for the lunch service around seven in the morning. Nothing out of the ordinary there. I couldn't come up with a single link between Carlos and Brent that made sense.

I didn't arrive at Sharon's house until four. She answered the door, her shirt dirty and the knees of her white leggings green from grass stains. She obviously didn't check the peephole, because the second it registered who I was she started yelling.

"What in the hell are you doing at my house? The one woman at that restaurant I trusted, and I find you were just another one of his fucks." She spat out the "k" with such force that a fine mist of spittle blanketed my face.

Never, for one minute, had it occurred to me that Sharon would think I'd slept with Brent. She glared at me with such pure venom that if she'd had a gun in her hand, she'd have killed me.

"Sharon, I was not having an affair with your husband. He and I respected each other in the kitchen, we worked well together, but that's it," I stressed. "I can't explain why he was killed in my house. Our relationship was strictly professional. Please believe me."

She stood there glowering at me, her arms wrapped tightly around her body, not willing to acknowledge anything I said.

I tried again. "I never would have gotten involved with him. Anyway, the bottom line is Brent wouldn't have been interested in me. I'm too old. He liked them…younger," I finished lamely, bringing a bitter smile to her face. Sharon knew that only too well.

"If you weren't having an affair with him, why was he in your bed?" she threw back at me. I guess the police had filled her in on the gory details.

"I don't know why, the police don't know why." In my final bid for forgiveness, I blurted out, "Sharon, for God's sake, my own marriage was destroyed because my husband fell in love with another woman. Do you think I'd in good conscience do that to someone else?"

I pushed all thoughts of that torrid scene with O'Connor aside.

Her voice lost its edge. "Brent never told me you and Jim split up."

"Couple of years ago. The divorce was final last year."

Typical of Brent. Here we'd worked together for more than seven years and it barely even registered with him that my world was falling apart.

"God, Brent was such a self-centered asshole. He never said a thing to me about you getting a divorce." Her body language relaxed. She rubbed her hands vigorously over her face and tied her long hair in a knot at the back of her neck.

"Come in, but I can't talk long. I need to make funeral arrangements before the kids get home from my mom's."

I followed her into the living room. It was gorgeous, just like I remembered from the magazine photo spread.

I knew Brent had used an interior designer, but obviously Sharon had made all the decisions. If Brent had had his heavy hand in it, the house would have been decorated in the most avant-garde Italy offered that year. Turquoise leather couches with cement slab coffee tables, that sort of thing.

Damask-covered couches, leather club chairs, and mahogany tables were placed artfully around the room. A baby grand, polished so black that I could see my face in it, graced one corner. This was the kind of room that begged for a fire, a good book, and a big snifter of brandy. She had capitulated on the artwork, it was outré and avant-garde. But the rest of the room was so inviting that the art was merely a minor irritation.

As I walked across the room, my shoes disappeared into an enormous Turkish rug that spanned the length and width of the room. I sat down in a leather club chair that swallowed me up; the nap of the leather caressed my back and neck, making me feel as if I were encased in a giant glove. I laid my arm flat against the arm of the chair so that the steak knife wouldn't prick the crook of my elbow.

Sharon parked herself across from me on a sofa that looked equally snug. Whatever skullduggery Brent was involved in, it certainly paid well. I thought about the furniture in my own house, mostly hand-me-downs from my parents. Why is honesty always either cheap or ugly?

"I'm very sorry. I...I know your marriage wasn't the best, but Brent's death must be very hard on your kids."

"Yes, it is." she closed her eyes briefly, exhaustion evident from the black circles under her eyes. "They're the only reason why I stayed with that two-timing bastard. They loved him and he loved them." She glanced at a montage of family photos on the wall next to the fireplace. Picture after picture cataloguing their life together, everyone smiling. One big happy family.

"Inspector O'Connor asked me if I was ever in the restaurant. I hated that goddamn restaurant. Every time I went in there I'd run into some beautiful twenty-year-old with a knowing smirk on her face. She'd look at me and gloat over my post-partum body. I was beautiful and slim at that age, too. I was such a lovely bride."

We automatically looked at their wedding pictures. Her face softened for a split second and I saw the girl she must have been without all that disappointment and anger carved deep into her features. "I believed in all that crap they feed you in the magazines. I actually thought that when we got married, he'd stop. Then I told myself once we had the kids he'd stop. It was all bullshit. I should have left. But when the kids were born and then they loved him so much, I couldn't leave. I thought that if you loved someone enough that everything would be okay." She looked at me with such longing that I knew she still wanted to believe it.

"It doesn't work that way," I said, thinking of my own photo album, now relegated to the box in the back of my hall closet.

"Why are you here, Mary?" Sharon asked, her voice back to its normal caustic tone. "I take it you didn't come here to discuss my lousy marriage."

"I think Brent and Carlos' murders are linked and that the restaurant is integral to the case."

She braced her hands against the seat like she was getting ready to stand up.

"You know I never interfered in the running of the restaurant. That was Brent's thing. I can't help you."

She was about to hoist herself up when I dropped the bombshell.

"Sharon, I was at the restaurant the night you and Brent went to the office."

Her hands went slack, her body retreated back into the folds of the couch. Her eyes jumped to the doorway and her butt wriggled in her seat, as if she were planning an escape route. Then her face smoothed over, confident and sure. She was going to call my bluff. "There wasn't anyone there, we checked," she challenged.

"Don't play poker with me." I wagged a finger at her. "I hold all the cards. You didn't check under Juan's desk. Want me to repeat verbatim your conversation? How did you say it? 'Your pride and joy? Spare me. You sure as hell didn't mind spending eighty hours here last week.'"

Sharon sat there stunned, many emotions playing across her face: surprise, fear, speculation, and lastly a grim determination. She didn't say anything for the longest time.

"You left the light on."

I nodded.

"I knew someone was there. Brent is an idiot." She slapped the arm of the couch in frustration; her voice berated Brent as if he weren't stiff and lifeless on an autopsy table. "Have you told the police?"

"Yes, I did. I'm sorry, Sharon," I apologized, "but I had no choice. Come clean with them. Right now Thom Woods is the prime suspect, but Thom has an alibi for Brent's murder. Once they find that out they'll be back to question you about the missing files. Play the long-suffering wife, the mother of his children. I think they'll go easy on you."

She leaned forward and put two surprisingly delicate hands on two rather fat knees.

"What's in this for you, Mary?"

The question surprised me. I didn't know the answer. Maybe I had to prove to O'Connor that I was as smart as I boasted I was or that we were equals. The answer I gave to Sharon acknowledged none of that.

"Someone tried to jimmy open the door to my motel room. He's killed two out of three. I don't want to make the third time a charm."

Her mouth fell open.

"Someone tried to kill you, too?"

"Yeah. I think these murders have something to do with the wine. Was Brent getting kickbacks?"

"I don't know." She leaned back into the couch. The damask crinkled as it adjusted to her weight.

"Sharon, it's a little too late in the game for this bullshit." I sounded angrier than I knew was wise, but I wanted answers and I wanted them now.

"I don't know the details. Really," she insisted. "Brent came home immediately after the police questioned him at the restaurant. He was hysterical. He kept repeating over and over again, 'The police are in the restaurant. They're searching everywhere.' Finally, it dawned on me that he wasn't hysterical, he was terrified."

"I picked up on that, too. His reaction to Carlos' murder was way over the top."

"We had the most awful fight of our whole marriage. And that's saying something. After I begged him for over an hour to tell me what was going on, he finally admitted that he and Juan were running an extremely lucrative scheme involving the wine. I went nuts, screaming how could he jeopardize our future with some stupid scam. I demanded some answers. He refused to say anything other than it involved wine. When I continued pressing him for details, it really got ugly."

She paused, closing her eyes in painful memory and her shoulders slumped further into the chair. I knew she was going to tell me everything. The air of confession was so strong I could eat it for dinner.

I prodded her. "What happened next, Sharon?"

"He started taunting me. How did I think we paid for this house, for the interior decorator and the expensive rugs on the floor and the kids' tuition at a fancy private school and the thousands of dollars a year I spent on plants. He began sneering about how I liked living the high life just as much as he did and I should shut up. When he told me to shut up, I grabbed a lamp and was about to throw it at him when you showed up. I probably would have killed him myself that night if you hadn't pounded on the window."

"That's the impression I got," I admitted.

"I love this house," she sighed and glanced around at the room, her eyes taking in every elegant curve, every tasteful artifact. "It will break my heart if we have to move, but right then and there I knew I couldn't live here on the proceeds of something illegal. The kids would adjust. I insisted we go to the restaurant and double-check that any incriminating paperwork had been destroyed. I got him to swear to me that he'd stop whatever he was doing. No more. Regardless of the financial outcome, it was going to stop."

Her face softened slightly.

"You have to understand, he grew up very poor. His father drank most of his paycheck. Sometimes Brent went to bed hungry. He started working in restaurants to get meals. Then he discovered that he had real talent, that he could actually make money cooking. And once he made money he had to buy expensive things to prove he wasn't poor. I've lost count of how many Italian leather jackets he bought himself. He was a weak man," she concluded.

"Was Thom involved?" I needed to cover all angles.

"Brent never mentioned Thom's name once. Besides, Brent thought he was a good controller but the guy has a perpetual bee up his ass." An apt description if ever I heard one. "Brent used him to butter up those socialites, but didn't like him much personally. Whatever was going on was between Brent and Juan."

"Are you sure you don't know anything more about it?" I wanted any pointless detail she could remember.

"No," she replied wearily. "All he told me was that it had something to do with the wine, nothing else. He refused. Said it was better that I didn't know."

Okay, now we're cooking with gas. This tied into what Teri Baxter had said. I leaned forward. "Do you know which winery is involved?"

"No. You heard me. When we got to the restaurant, Juan had erased everything on the computer and was going to manufacture fake invoices to cover up the fact that the shipments had arrived."

"Sharon, do you have any idea who would want to kill Brent?"

She laughed, a mean, nasty laugh. "Oh please, Mary. I naturally assumed a woman had done it. When I found out that it happened in your house, I was surprised. You're right, he liked 'em young. But to be honest, I'd come to the point where I believed the man would fuck anything female. Except me," she whispered, with tears in her eyes.

She still loved him. He humiliated her with bimbo after bimbo, and she still loved him.

Sharon began rubbing her eyes. "I'm so tired, you can't believe how tired I am." Then she looked straight at me. "I'm sorry for my kids, they'll really miss him, but you don't know how bone weary I am. I wasn't like this before. Maybe now I can get back my self-respect and focus on taking care of them. At least Brent was insured, and if I sell the restaurant we should be fine. Anyway, you want details about the wine, grill Juan. He had Brent completely under his thumb. He's an evil man."

I couldn't believe my ears.

"This is Juan Vamos we're talking about, right?" I needed to make sure. There was no way to candy coat the word "evil." Was my internal radar so amiss that I'd missed the true nature of Juan's personality?

"He's a snake. Do you wonder why your restaurant runs so well? He threatens the staff with their jobs and makes them work overtime with no pay. If any of them make any noise, they're fired, and good luck in finding another job. Juan blackballs them. Brent wanted to fire him, but depended on him too much."

All these years I assumed the deferential attitude the staff displayed toward Juan was respect; now I find it was abject fear.

Memo to self: learn Spanish in the New Year.

"Brent let him do this?" I was incredulous. Brent might have fucked his way through countless women, but he was a scrupulously fair employer.

"He tried to stop him, but Juan did it behind his back. If Brent found out about any overtime, he'd give people money under the table. The threats and blackballing he couldn't do anything about."

I was speechless. O'Connor was right. You could work with people for years and not know anything about them.

"Now, please, Mary, I need to make arrangements for Brent's funeral."

Like beached whales trying to get back to water, we heaved ourselves out of our seats and headed for the front door.

"Sharon, one more thing. Do you think Juan's capable of murder?"

Without a moment's hesitation, she said flatly, "In a New York minute."

Chapter 20

I drove around the block, parked my car, and then ripped the tape off my arm and threw the steak knife on the passenger floorboard. I needed to think, balancing what I knew against what I didn't know. Given: Brent and Juan were in on the wine deal together. Who else? Cross out Drew, Teri, and Sharon. Thom? Sharon said no, but the new BMW and fancy address said yes. Thom wasn't available—this very second O'Connor was roasting him over hot coals. That left Gilberto.

I pulled into the parking lot of San Francisco General and headed to the information desk to find out Gilberto's status. S.F. General was, unfortunately, all too familiar territory. Two years ago Amos had wasted down to a hundred and twenty pounds and had been fighting leprosy in addition to AIDS. I spent many hours here keeping him company while they poked and probed, trying to stop that evil virus from destroying him. Then the FDA approved the cocktail. His recovery has been amazing; he's a poster boy for the drug companies.

The pink ladies told me Gilberto had been moved out of intensive care to the fifth floor. My luck held until I got off the elevator and made my way down the corridor. A police guard sat in front of Gilberto's door reading a magazine.

Time for Plan B. I made a U-turn and went to a pay phone near the elevator bank and tried to ring Gilberto's room. He wasn't allowed any phone calls either. O'Connor was too efficient for me.

I've been around hospitals all my life. My dad was a doctor, my mother a nurse. As a kid I hung about the back corridors of emergency rooms and surgical units. I know how hospitals work. Time for Plan C.

I checked my watch and scanned the ward. I had a plan. It was just after five-thirty, but I didn't see any sign of the dinner carts. This might work.

I took the elevator down to the fourth floor. Eureka. Halfway down the corridor stood a rack half filled with dinner trays. I checked the nursing station; one nurse was on the phone writing on a chart, the other was watching a monitor. I hoped that if they noticed me, the white chef's jacket would fool them into thinking I was a doc. A uniform does two things: first, it makes you invisible. If I'm wearing chef's whites it takes forever to be waited on in a store. Second, it gives you an identity.

Sweating buckets from the adrenaline racing through my veins, I walked quietly over to the rack and without a sound, slid out one tray. I half expected someone to stop me, but no one noticed. I carried the tray to the elevator without a hitch and went back up to the fifth floor.

Now the hard part. The cop guarding the door looked like he had just graduated from the Academy. His shoes and badge were shined to perfection, suggesting his uniform hadn't yet lost its allure. He didn't have a nametag, but I was betting it would be something like Riordan or O'Sullivan. The red hair and blue eyes were a dead giveaway. Time to play the Irish card.

"Hello, Officer," I beamed. "How's it going? My name's Moira O'Connor, I'm the Chief Dietician here at S.F. General. I have Mr. Perez's dinner. Okay if I go on in?"

"Ms. O'Connor did you say?" His eyes searched my jacket for a nametag.

I nodded and smiled, working those Irish dimples overtime in an effort to make up for the lack of identification.

"Perez gets his food before everyone else? They didn't tell me that."

"Glycine allergy," I lied. "If he has anything except vegetables or fruits he breaks out in gigantic pustules all over his body, poor man." I tsked several times. "I know an Irish face when I see one," I teased. "Let me guess. You look like an O'Shaunessy to me."

"Powers, actually, ma'am."

I looked at him in faux amazement. "That's my grandmother's maiden name. Wouldn't surprise me if we were related somehow."

I smiled that little smirk of conspiracy that the Irish give to one another.

He hesitated for a moment, checking out the uniform and the food tray.

"I guess it's okay. Don't be too long."

"Quick as a bunny," I assured him. I felt a surge of triumph. The nuns never told me lying could be so much fun.

I'd have to move fast. Even that novice would get suspicious if I stayed in Gilberto's room too long.

Luckily he had a private room. I stashed the food tray on his bedside table and then wove my way through the various machines surrounding his bedside to monitor his vital signs. Everything seemed to be beeping in a steady rhythm. Hopefully he wouldn't need any nursing assistance in the next five minutes.

Gilberto was asleep but he must have been having a nightmare. His brow was deeply furrowed, giving a sneak preview of what he'd look like as an old man. I put a hand on his thin shoulder and shook him gently.

"Gilberto, it's Mary, Mary Ryan, from the restaurant," I whispered. "Wake up. I need to ask you a few questions."

He opened his eyes slowly, as if he were a vampire and the light from the bedside table were an instrument of torture.

"*Señora*?" he asked and then fell back into a foggy stupor.

Dammit, I hadn't counted on him being so drugged.

"Gilberto, wake up," I said louder this time and tickled his cheek.

His eyes opened again and tried to focus in my direction.

"Gilberto, this is very important. Was Thom Woods mixed up in the wine scam at the restaurant?"

"No, not Mr. Woods. Juan." The drugs made his speech slurred and thick. It was almost impossible to understand him.

"Were you involved?"

He closed his eyes again and nodded yes. "Only to protect Carlitos. He needed money. Juan *malo*. Evil. You stay away from him."

My knight in shining armor.

His face went slack; he had nodded off again. I pinched the web between his thumb and index finger. "Gilberto, stay awake. Mr. Woods. What's he doing at the restaurant? Something illegal?"

"Mishter Woods?"

I leaned over and gently squeezed both his cheeks.

"Mr. Woods, Gilberto. What was he doing that was illegal?"

"Makes green cards. Can't go to police. Not legal. Send us back to El Salvador. Me. Rosa."

Restaurants used to automatically look the other way when they hired Latinos. You assumed they were illegal. Then about fifteen years ago the Feds offered the iron fist in the velvet glove. The glove meant amnesty for those who could prove they'd been in the country for a number of years. A lot of illegals got green cards through this program. The iron fist was that it was now the legal burden of the business community to make sure that the people they hired were legit. This created a whole new market for bogus green cards

Things were falling into place. I felt a smug satisfaction. First, Thom's new car and the expensive apartment, then Gilberto's reluctance to talk to the police. The color of his skin and heavy accent would immediately trigger a check on his immigration status. If he was deported, who was going to support his family back in El Salvador? Gilberto's palpable frustration that afternoon at Rosa's place now made sense.

Thom, you slag heap of putrid lamb fat. You paid for that fancy new car off the backs of people making eight bucks an hour. What in the hell is Amos doing with this man?

Memo to self: Ask him.

I brushed Gilberto's hair away from his face. "You take care. I'll be back in a couple of days when you're feeling better." Gilberto grunted and then fell back asleep.

I exited the room and closed the door behind me without making a sound. Looking at Officer Powers, I put a finger up to my lips, indicating quiet.

"He's asleep," I said in a mock whisper. "I'll wake him up in a little while."

I sauntered slowly down the hospital corridor and nonchalantly pushed the elevator button. I was so nervous beads of sweat dribbled down my back. It wasn't until I reached the parking lot that I allowed myself a gargantuan sigh of relief.

I paged O'Connor. While waiting for him to call me back, I rehearsed various scenarios in my head, searching for the right tone to adopt with him. I must be detached, professional, and above all, not mention that scene in his car.

"Ryan."

That was it. Just my name. The bastard was putting the ball in my court. Two can play that game.

"O'Connor."

Silence.

"Where are you?"

"I'm just getting off the freeway," I lied. "I'm passing S.F. General right now. I just talked to Amos and…"

He cut me off. "Meet me at the restaurant in ten minutes. If you get there before I do, lock your doors and wait for me. Don't move."

I pulled out of the S.F. General parking lot and was heading down Army when a number of loud, insistent honks got my attention. I looked in the rearview mirror. A blue van muscled its way out of the S.F. General parking lot and began weaving in and out of rush-hour traffic. Trying to catch up to me.

My stomach dropped to the floorboard in a panic. I'd heard on the radio two weeks earlier that the worst mistake a woman can make is to ignore her instincts in potentially dangerous situations. My instincts were screaming loud and clear. This time I wasn't going to take any chances.

I leaned over and scooped the steak knife off the floor and placed it on the seat next to me. Then I called 911.

"My name is Mary Ryan. There's someone following me in a blue van. The windows are," I gasped for air, "dark and I can't see the license plate, but a…a…a…this guy's been," I took another couple of deep breaths, "stalking me for a couple of days. What should I do?" It was difficult to talk. Fear was choking off my oxygen. I rolled the window down, letting the cold October night air fill the car. If I didn't get more air I was going to pass out.

"Ma'am, you're calling from a cell phone, right? All cell phones are routed to the CHP. Give me your exact location."

Cell phones are the 911 dispatchers' bane of existence.

"I'm at Army and Potrero. He's three cars behind me."

"Okay, turn right onto Potrero. Is he still following you?"

I checked the mirror. Yep. It was rush hour, so there were plenty of cars for cover. He was able to keep a safe distance between us.

"Y…y…yeah." My teeth were chattering. I'd never been so afraid. "He's still there."

"What kind of car is it?"

"A light blue, late model Chevy van. One of the longer types."

"Okay, Ma'am. Listen closely. What kind of car are you driving?"

"A 1986 Subaru wagon, beige, license plate number 582 SHY."

"Drive slowly. The Potrero Street Station is at the corner of Connecticut and Potrero. I'm going to have someone contact S.F.P.D. right now. Stay on the line. Hear me? There'll be a couple of cruisers waiting for you to drive by the station. They'll corner the van with their cars. Got that?"

"Y…y…yes," I stuttered.

That drive to the Potrero Street Station was the longest drive of my life. The traffic had thinned out so it was only him and me. The van kept me in its sight, but stayed several car lengths behind. As I got closer to the police station, he started to slow down, realizing where I was headed. It was too late. Two cruisers squealed out of the side streets, blocking Potrero. Two more cruisers came up from behind the van at breakneck speed with their lights flashing and pinned him from that direction. He was trapped.

I stopped my car in the middle of the street, got out, and hid behind a telephone pole in case there was any gunfire. I didn't trust that sardine can car of mine to stop any bullets. I peeked around the pole to see who it was—the person who had murdered Carlos and Brent.

Four officers leaped out of their cars, three of them with their guns drawn. The fourth officer cupped a radio-operated megaphone in her hand and ordered the driver to exit the car, hands over his head.

He got out of the car.

I screamed at him, "You fucking idiot."

It was Jim, his badge held high in the air.

Chapter 21

I kept mute while Jim explained to his fellow officers why he had been stalking his ex-wife for the last three days. I wasn't going to sabotage him, but I certainly had no intention of making it any easier.

At some point they got O'Connor on the phone, who explained that Jim wasn't actually stalking me. O'Connor, concerned about my safety as the lead witness to two homicides, gave Jim permission to keep an eye on me because the department didn't have funds for a tail. Next, Jim started telling a few jokes, and pretty soon everyone was slapping each other on the back and laughing about Jim nearly getting his head blown off. Failing to see the humor in the situation, I went and sat in my car, taking deep breaths in an effort to bring my pulse down to normal and stop my hands from shaking.

After yucking it up for a few more minutes, the cops got into their cruisers and drove off. Jim shuffled over to the Subaru, his hands in his pockets, his face flushed with embarrassment. He began to walk around the car, as if to get into the passenger's seat and then saw the expression on my face and stopped.

"Mary, I'm really sorry," he apologized.

"You were way out of bounds." I struggled to stay calm. "Pick up the newspapers lately? Sickos abducting women right, left, and center. You're lucky I didn't shoot you."

He laughed. "You? You wouldn't even let me have guns in the house when we were married."

"Stop laughing," I ordered. My jaw was clenched so tight that I could barely enunciate. "I've never been so terrified in my life."

"I'm sorry, you weren't supposed to see me. It's just that O'Connor and I, well, we were worried about you. You're so goddamn independent. You wouldn't stay with your mother. Can't you understand that you could be in real danger?"

"That doesn't give you the right to stalk me." I leaned against the steering wheel and took several more deep breaths.

"Can I get in?" he asked.

I shook my head. I opened both front doors and leaned back, trying to get as much air into my lungs as possible. Slowly my pulse eased its way back to normal.

After about five minutes, Jim slipped inside and sat down. "Are you okay?"

"Yes," I replied. I sat up straight and looked at him. "I say this not to be mean or nasty, but I'm not your business anymore, Jim. We're done."

He shook his head. "Mary, you're still my business. If I was hurt or killed in the line of duty, would it mean nothing to you?"

I said nothing but stared down Potrero, lined with old cars and abandoned industrial hangars.

"We might be divorced, but ten years is ten years. There are reasons why it didn't work. And it's not just the baby. Maybe I didn't end it nicely, but it was over. Even if Tina wasn't in the picture. We didn't have much left. It's the idea of me rather than me, isn't it?"

Liar, I wanted to scream at him, but somehow I couldn't. I flashed on Sharon Brown sitting in her tastefully appointed living room, with grass-stained pants and dirty hair, and so much anger and bitterness in her heart that her only hope for redemption was in her husband's death.

All of a sudden all that energy I'd expended in the last two years hating him seemed more self-destructive than anything else. It was time to release him—release myself.

"Is that Tina's car?" I gestured in the direction of the blue van.

"Yeah. I told you, she and the kids are out of town. Do you think we could just talk to each other every now and then? Just to check and see how you're doing. Your folks. Nora and Dan."

He was so sweet and gentle, too gentle to be a cop. That sideways grin of his, the reddish-brown mop of hair, the blue eyes. I used to fantasize that our children would have his sense of humor, his smile, and my green eyes, my intellect, my drive.

"Come on, Miss Mary, Mary Quite Contrary."

"Don't call me that," I whispered. That was his special little phrase he used over the years to tease me out of bad moods, political rants about the injustices of the world, and general ill humor. Since our divorce I had, indeed, become quite contrary.

"I'm sorry. That was out of line," he said, pushing himself out of the car and quietly shutting the passenger door. "I just want to say hi now and then. That's all."

"Maybe. No. I don't know, Jim. Call me in a couple of weeks. I've got to meet O'Connor at the restaurant." I closed my door, put the car in gear and sped off, not wanting to hear any more. I watched him in the rearview mirror watching me. I turned at the first corner I could.

It was after eight by the time I made it to the restaurant. The fog had done its slinky dance through the Golden Gate; the alley glistened with the kind of fresh fog that creeps up your pant legs and makes you shiver. Winter was coming.

When I pulled up, O'Connor jumped out of his car. I didn't even look at him. I headed for the front door of the restaurant, disabled the alarm, unlocked the restaurant, and sat down at a large table for eight. O'Connor picked up the hint and seated himself across the way.

"I expect an official apology from you, Inspector O'Connor. How dare you have me tailed without my permission? I'm two seconds away from reporting you to the Police Commission." My anger had regenerated itself on the drive from the police station to the restaurant. I was mad enough to carve my initials on his forehead with a butter knife.

Instead of an apology, I got another reprimand.

"Your behavior today is exactly why I had Jim tailing you. Why aren't you still at your mother's house?"

"After my mother so generously offered Teri Baxter my old bedroom for the night, where did you think I was going to stay? You know that house has only two bedrooms. Didn't hear an invitation leaping from your lips. My house is still off limits—the forensic boys have it trussed up in crime scene tape. I'm staying with Amos for a few days."

"And how do Sharon Brown and San Francisco General figure into this equation?" He picked up a salt shaker, rolled it between his hands, and then slammed it hard on the table. "You're still running around like a chicken without a head. Mary, two people are dead and you came close to being number three."

He started shouting.

"I don't know what to do with you. What if you had stumbled in on those guys as they were trashing Teri's studio? My God, I couldn't live with myself if you had been—" then his head nodded forward. Without lifting his head, he whispered, "Please listen to me. When I ask you to call me, call me. When I tell you to go straight home, go straight home. I'm not asking you as a homicide inspector, I'm begging you as...." He left the sentence unfinished. That, of course, was the $64,000 question. As what?

"All right," I whispered back.

He stretched his hand across the table for my hand. I reached for his, but the table was too big, our hands were marooned in the middle. We looked at each other. The same confusion, guilt, and sadness I felt on my own face I saw on his.

After a few seconds he removed his hand.

"What's next?" I asked quietly.

"The subpoenas were a bust. Drew gets ten thou every month from some trust fund, and by the thirtieth of every month it's spent out. That got me hot and bothered, but when I checked Brent's bank accounts they looked okay. He must have some accounts his wife doesn't know about or he paid for all his toys in cash. Hunting for those hidden accounts will take time. For now that leaves Woods. You know Woods has an alibi?"

I nodded. "Amos told me."

"Seems Amos is his alibi for Brent's murder. What Amos doesn't know is that his boyfriend is not in the clear by a long shot."

I winced at the word "boyfriend."

"Woods is running a little green card factory out of here."

"Oh, really?" I tried to sound surprised. I didn't want to get that cute young cop in trouble. I'd wait and see how much information O'Connor wrung out of Thom and then decide if Gilberto's revelations were relevant. If O'Connor found out I'd finagled my way into Gilberto's room, that guy's next job would be as a security guard at a Target store.

"Apparently he'd stay after hours and print the cards up late at night. We've turned him over to the INS, assuming no further leads tie him in with Perez's murder."

"Have you questioned him?"

"Yeah. He admits to the green card fraud, but staunchly denies any connection to the murders. Looks like almost every Latino at the restaurant has fake I.D. He charges two thousand bucks a card and not just for the employees in this place. We have a nice little list of at least two hundred illegals he's printed out I.D.'s for."

Slime bucket.

"Did you check out the taqueria?"

"Yeah, nothing. The neighbors told us that the day you nearly got your head sliced open was the last day it was open and no one's been back since. The owner of the building says they rented from month to month and always paid in cash. No paper trail."

"I talked to Sharon Brown this afternoon," I said. "She told me that Juan Vamos was Brent's partner in the scam. Thom wasn't in the picture at all."

O'Connor rubbed his hands over his face.

"But Vamos has an alibi. Christ, I'm tired. Do you think there's any connection between Woods's green card operation and Brent's wine scam?"

I'd been trying to make a connection between the two during the entire drive from S.F. General to the restaurant.

"No. Sharon was emphatic that the wine scam was Brent and Juan's gig. The only possible connection I see is that Carlos was helping Juan and Brent and that he also had a fake green card from Thom, but that doesn't implicate Thom in the wine deal."

"I questioned Woods for several hours. The guy's a real piece of work. Made all kinds of noises that he was going to rally the gay community behind him to stop this police harassment. Fortunately, INS showed up and educated Woods on the reality of counterfeiting. Like a million years in a federal penitentiary. I didn't like him but he's not capable of murder. I agree with you."

"That's a first." I couldn't resist.

"Cut the smart-ass remarks, Ryan. Let's start at the beginning. How did Teri get pulled into this? The only connection I can think of is that Smyth-Sommers woman. She knew about Teri blabbing about the scam because you told her."

"I think it's bigger than that. Rosa knew Carlos was involved in something, but she didn't have a clue what it was, other than suspecting it was connected to his murder. I don't think we can assume Drew is our only link to Teri. If Carlos' murder is related to the wine scam, Brent might have told Juan that Teri knew."

"What did Sharon Brown have to say?"

"Sharon told me that Brent and Juan ran the scam together. She and Brent had a big fight the day I discovered the body. Brent admitted he and Juan were in cahoots, but he refused to give her any details. Maybe he was protecting her. Brent knew and look where it got him."

"You believe her?"

"Yeah, I do. What if Carlos threatened Brent and Juan with exposure or wanted a cut of the pie, so they killed him? Once everything started heating up, Juan knew that Brent would cave in so Juan killed him too," I theorized. "But why would a lowly little pastry assistant like Carlos be part of a kickback scheme?"

O'Connor stood up.

"I'm going to ignore the green card thing and assume that both these murders tie into the wine. Any bright ideas how we can track down this specific wine? I boxed up all the wine invoices that forensics removed when they hauled away the file cabinets. They only go back a year, but it's something. They're in my car. But what we're going to do with them, I haven't a clue. I'll be back in a minute."

While O'Connor went out to his car, I recalled everything Brent had said to Sharon the night they surprised me in the office. Juan had erased the computer records, but hadn't made up the fake invoices yet. The wine wasn't on the menu, but it did come in with other wine shipments. So if the invoices hadn't been switched yet, then the wine would be on the invoice but *not* on the wine list.

"Here," said O'Connor, throwing a box on the table. "Take this upstairs. There's one more in the car. I'll meet you up there. Any bright ideas?"

"Oh, I think so. Although it will only work if you guys hauled away the file cabinets before Juan could replace the fake invoices."

I grabbed a couple of wine lists from the waiters' station and made my way upstairs to the office.

Wine sales are the real moneymaker in a restaurant. American Fare offers more than two hundred selections, excluding champagnes, ports, spirits and aperitifs. Why do you think corkage fees are so outrageous? To discourage you from drinking anything but what we stock. If your restaurant buys wine at ten dollars a bottle wholesale, they are going to charge you between twenty-five and thirty retail. Wine doesn't have to be chopped, cooked, braised, or whipped. All a waiter has to do is remove the cork and pour.

"What's the plan?" puffed O'Connor, as he dropped the second box at my feet.

I grinned. "Looks to me like Juan didn't get here in time. All the invoices look genuine in my box. Unfortunately, there's no way of knowing if he's pulled them completely, but we'll have to take that chance. Your computer forensic guys might be able to salvage the erased stuff off of the hard drive, but until then we have no way of knowing whether these are complete or not."

I was sitting on the floor piling invoices into two stacks. My hands were black from carbon residue. "Let's limit the search to only those brokers who specialize in South American and Spanish wine. If Juan's involved, there's a good chance it's a Latino connection."

"Which would make sense with Carlos' murder," O'Connor agreed.

"Once we segregate out these brokers, we'll compare the items on the invoices with the wine list. Because Sharon said the wine wasn't on the menu, we'll look for the wine *not* included on the wine list. Although not every wine we have in the cellar is on the wine list, it should narrow it down, or at the very least, give you a starting point on which broker to target. It can't be the wine itself. It doesn't make sense. It must be the name of the broker we're after. If the current batch of brokers turns up bust, we'll move on to another broker."

Halfway through my stack I began to get hunger pangs.

"I need something to eat, O'Connor. Can I get you something from the kitchen?" He made a grunt in my direction. I assumed that meant yes. A gooey, hot omelet sounded just about perfect.

I whipped up those omelets in no time and was putting the dirty sauté pans in the sink when I hit my leg against a rack of glasses. I felt the old cut on my leg burst open. Shit, shit, shit. I limped over to the first aid station to stem the flow of blood and was throwing the tape back into the cabinet when it dawned on me. That guy with the dolly that ran into me wasn't making a delivery, he was taking wine out of the restaurant.

Why in the hell would someone be taking wine out of the restaurant?

Maybe it wasn't wine in those bottles.

I grabbed some silverware with one hand, balanced the plates on the other, and ran to the office screaming, "O'Connor, O'Connor, it's not kickbacks. I know what I forgot to tell you."

"And what was that, Mary?" Juan purred.

Chapter 22

Juan stood next to O'Connor, a gun six inches from his head. O'Connor's hands were laced behind the back of his neck, the gun holster under his arm empty.

"I can't believe my luck," Juan smiled. "To catch you and Inspector O'Connor. The gods are smiling on me tonight."

I stood there balancing the plates with one hand, clutching silverware with the other. I stared at the gun poised to blow a hole in O'Connor's skull.

"I see I have your attention, Mary. Guns look so much more menacing in real life," Juan commented.

I moved my eyes a fraction of an inch to O'Connor's face. We locked eyes. I saw fear and anger. "Talk" he mouthed to me silently.

"What's in those wine bottles, Juan? What exactly were you removing that day? Is that why you got so mad at that delivery guy? He wasn't making a delivery, was he? He was removing wine."

"I wondered when that would occur to you. I told Brent you weren't stupid, that you would remember eventually, but he dismissed it. I see now he was trying to protect you. In fact, Mary, you have been most impressive throughout this whole affair."

I waited for some signal from O'Connor. His face was like stone. I goaded Juan further. "Well, let's make an educated guess. Something that could be put in a bottle. Drugs, maybe?"

"Correct, again. Cocaine. It's quite an operation. We make sure that none of the cases is heavier than the others, the dogs can't sniff it, and we are very careful not to make the whole shipment with doctored bottles. Only two cases in fifteen have contraband in them and some shipments have none," he chuckled. "It's been very successful. Too successful to let a cocky little prep cook ruin it for us."

"So you ran a drug smuggling operation out of one of the top five restaurants in the country with no one the wiser. Pretty damn clever," I conceded. "I suppose Carlos was blackmailing you?"

"Yes," he sighed. "Carlos got a little greedy. He threatened to expose us if we didn't give him a bigger cut. I think the pressure of another baby made him reckless. He supported quite a large family in El Salvador as well. Needless to say, you weren't supposed to find him. He was going to be removed early that morning. No one would question a janitor hauling a laundry bag out the door. Carlos needed to be made an example of. If I had let him take an inch, the others would have taken a mile."

It was as if he were talking about errant schoolboys leaving fingerprints on the walls.

"Others," I repeated. "It was someone from the restaurant who trashed Teri Baxter's apartment. She thought their voices sounded familiar."

"Yes. Again, you were at the right place at the right time. That silly girl would have kept her mouth shut if you hadn't rescued her. I sent them back to make sure she understood my message, but when they returned they saw you speeding away with her in your car."

Don't panic. Ignore the gun. Keep him talking, I told myself. He might let his guard down and give O'Connor a chance.

"Why did you kill Brent?" I demanded.

"I am sorry about Brent, we go back a long way," Juan admitted. "But if there's one person Brent was more afraid of than me it was Sharon. She had the *cojones* in that family."

His voice was thick with contempt. "I couldn't rely on him anymore. He came crying to me that he'd promised Sharon he wouldn't front the drugs anymore. He begged me to let him out of it. I saw the writing on the wall. Once the police started questioning him, he would have confessed in five minutes and begged for mercy. Being a nice white boy, he'd have gotten off with a slap on the wrists. Me, I'd be in Pelican Bay for the rest of my life. Why do you think I followed Brent from restaurant to restaurant? No one hires Latinos like me for any job higher than line cook."

"But why the drugs?" I was genuinely puzzled. "Both of you were well paid."

"I don't think working a seventy-hour week and making sixty thousand a year is really worth it, do you? I wanted the big money," he said simply. "That was the one thing Brent and I had in common. My mother worked like a dog to send me to the Jesuits. I was malnourished, but very well educated. Why do you think I speak English so well? Those priests beat proper Spanish and English into me. I had half a mind to become a Jesuit, they lead a very pampered life in Mexico."

O'Connor moved his right elbow a millimeter.

Juan moved the gun until it was two inches from O'Connor's head.

"Don't move a muscle, Inspector O'Connor." He turned back to me. "Brent and I were both very ambitious, something Sharon could never understand. Right away Brent and I realized we made a good team. Where do you think Brent got the money to open American Fare? Our colleagues in Chile fronted him the money."

"Vino Blanco Corporation," I said flatly.

Juan looked at me with unconcealed admiration.

"You should hire this woman, Inspector. She's run rings around your department." The fact that he was handing me bouquets of compliments didn't give me any hope he wasn't going to shoot me where I stood. "I was most alarmed when Pepe told me you showed up at the taqueria. Brent forced me to put Vino Blanco on the business license. Something about taxes and how if Vino Blanco didn't put up the money he would be audited and our operation would crumble."

"But Vino Blanco's not real," I said.

"Of course it's real. We operate a legitimate wine import/ export business. Brent had to have an official source for the start-up costs. It seemed a small concession at the time. How was I to know that you, Mary Ryan, would discover the one piece of paper that linked Vino Blanco to American Fare. It was a perfect plan. I had a little trouble convincing Brent to go in with me, but the lure of opening his own place was too tempting."

Sharon was right, Juan was evil. Except for the hand pointing the gun at O'Connor's head, his manner was nonchalant, as if we were discussing a minor etiquette faux pas, like using the cheese fork for your dessert.

"And you killed him in my bedroom because he was losing his nerve. Right?"

He nodded. "I toyed with the idea of framing him for Carlos' murder but couldn't quite see making that work. I kept an eye on him, followed him to your house, and confronted him. He was waiting for you to return from Carlos' funeral. He planned on confessing the whole thing to you. Brent hoped that you'd speak on his behalf to your ex-husband and try to cut him a deal. You really should get better locks. We walked right in. Where were you? I had a lovely murder-suicide plan all mapped out. I really didn't care whether they believed you murdered him or he committed suicide, he had to be silenced."

That silly indulgence in vanity saved my life. The next time I had an impulse for a manicure I was going to give into it with a vengeance.

"How did you get his clothes and toiletries into my house?"

"Drew was very helpful in that regard. She had several articles of Brent's clothing and things at her place and provided the 'props,' shall we say. It was, and is, a good plan. Carlos will be dismissed as a victim of some Latino in-fighting, Brent the victim of some love affair gone wrong." He smiled at O'Connor. "The police like everything simple, don't they, Inspector?"

O'Connor's moved his chin a fraction of an inch, as if to silently challenge that last statement.

"Uh, uh, uh, Inspector." Juan moved the gun toward O'Connor's head another half inch. "I suggest you stay still. Any false moves on your part and who knows? I might get confused and our lovely Mary might get in the way of the confusion."

"Is Drew involved in this?" I demanded, in an attempt to draw Juan's attention away from O'Connor and back to me.

"Oh, yes. Beautiful Drew." Juan smiled. "She and her rich friends like cocaine, especially since it's laced with heroin. Tames the beast, so they tell me. They buy out every shipment. She gets a nice percentage, of course."

"But she doesn't need the money," I protested. I thought about the outfit she'd worn that night I ambushed her in her doorway. Her monogrammed mules probably cost more than all my shoes put together.

"Oh, sad little story there. I think Drew needs all the money she can get. She's developing a nasty little habit. She told me what you said about Teri. She was so angry," he laughed. "She wanted me to kill Teri right away, but I said no. In hindsight she was right."

Because I always felt like I had permanent food stains on my clothes around Drew, I'd been overjoyed to think that she wasn't in the loop for once. Naturally, she was the very center of the loop. She was angry because Brent had jeopardized their little enterprise by his bedroom whisperings to Teri, not because Teri was privy to info she didn't have.

I fingered the plate of eggs, debating whether or not to risk throwing it in Juan's face. As though he could read my mind, O'Connor moved his eyes back and forth a fraction of a millimeter. No, not yet.

"But if you were going to implicate me, why attack me in the motel room?"

"Unfortunately, once you found out about the wine, I knew I'd have to kill you, too. I had a meeting arranged with Drew that night. We were going to talk about what to do next. I saw you leaving her house. She told me that you knew about the wine. I followed you to the motel. I had hoped to make it look like a random attack, but again luck was with you. That was pretty smart, trying to cut up the credit card. You are strong," he admitted. "It was too bad that Gilberto Perez got in my way."

I'd managed to keep the fear at bay up until now, but screams were pushing up against my throat. All these confessions on his part were just the entree. Clearly, dessert meant pumping multitudes of bullets into O'Connor and me. Despite all his talking, Juan remained in complete control, never flinching or relaxing the gun pointed at O'Connor's head.

O'Connor must have seen the panic mounting on my face. The grim mask he'd worn since I'd entered the room softened a little and his eyes seemed to say, Hold on, Mary, hold on.

"Don't kill us, Vamos," O'Connor warned. "You'll never get away with four murders."

"Yes, I will, Inspector." This man was going to kill us as casually as you'd throw a lobster into boiling water. "Your deaths will be ascribed to a robbery gone awry. I'll rifle through the safe, take some liquor. I'll make it look authentic. I doubt the police will suspect me. I live in Pacific Heights, I drive a fifty-thousand-dollar Mercedes, and I have a Swiss bank account. I don't think you two are going to stop me. Shall we kill the Inspector first, Mary?"

O'Connor blinked twice very fast. I hurled the plate of cold wet eggs and silverware in their direction and trusted that O'Connor would be expecting it and duck.

As I flew through the doorway, I heard a gun go off. I said a silent prayer to the Virgin Mary.

Don't let it be O'Connor.

I ran down the stairs toward the front door, my feet never so light and nimble in my life. Halfway across the dining room I heard heavy footsteps following me down the stairs. I knew I'd never make it to the front door. He'd shoot me right in the back. I raced behind the bar. In the big mirror over the bar I saw Juan enter the dining room.

I did some quick thinking. If I could see Juan, could he see me? No. With Brent's meticulous eye, he'd never position the bar mirror so that you'd see the bartender's feet while he was fixing your drink. Fortunately, the floor was covered with heavy rubber matting.

Making no sound, I crawled across the floor of the bar. I kept my eyes on Juan as I inched my way toward the far wall. If I could get to the podium near the front door, I could call 911 on the reservation telephone. I prayed that the tables, still covered with linens, were close enough together so he wouldn't see me scuttling across the floor.

He scanned the dining room, poised. Suddenly, I heard a big thump overhead. O'Connor.

Juan remained where he was for a second, and then started back toward the office stairs. When he reached the staircase, I got up from my hiding place behind the bar and hurled a glass tumbler across the dining room and into the open kitchen. It worked. Juan raced into the kitchen, and I ran for the podium. I grabbed the phone, crouched back on the floor behind a table, and frantically dialed 911.

I reached an operator and whispered as loud as I dared, "Cop down, cop shot," knowing that would get them here like lightning.

The operator started speaking loudly into the phone, demanding to know if the cop was okay. Her voice carried through the silent restaurant. I slammed down the receiver. I looked in the mirror. Juan had turned around and was looking directly at the podium. The phone was missing. A little smile played on his lips.

I had to get away from that phone. Fast. I began crawling between the tables, never once taking my eyes off that mirror.

I realized too late that I had crawled far enough into the dining room that I was now visible in the bar mirror. Our eyes locked.

He called my name: "Mary." His voice was soft and gentle like a lover.

My only salvation was to anticipate when he was going to shoot and heave a chair at him at just the right moment in the hope of throwing him off the mark. He was ten tables away and coming closer. Eight tables away. Six. At four tables away, he flexed the biceps of the arm holding the gun. He was going to shoot me from there.

I jumped to my feet and grabbed the closest chair. I hoisted it to my chest and was about to throw it up in the air when I heard several quick explosions in a row. Blood spewed all over the white tablecloths.

Oh dear Jesus, he hit me.

I began patting my white chef's jacket frantically trying to stop the flow of blood.

But it wasn't me.

The force of the bullets had propelled Juan forward and pitched him onto one of the dining tables. Beneath his splayed body, a halo of blood stained the white tablecloth, growing in ever-widening circles.

O'Connor leaned against the wall of the staircase, one arm wrapped around his torso, the other holding a gun.

Chapter 23

O'Connor's bulletproof vest saved our lives. He was shot at such close range that it broke three ribs, but luckily the bullets didn't penetrate his vest. Those police-issued, nine-millimeter Glock semi-automatics mean business. Juan was dead on impact.

We never did find out where Brent was the night of Carlos' murder. Sharon confirmed that he didn't come home until three that night, but no one believed he helped kill Carlos. O'Connor and I surmised that Juan had Drew set up a romantic tryst with Brent that evening so that he could kill Carlos without Brent interfering.

Naturally, Drew denied knowing anything about the drug smuggling. She hired the biggest legal guns in the city and didn't have to appear in court once. I've heard through the grapevine that she's in a major detox facility back east.

Gilberto vanished from the hospital two days before he was due to be discharged. Rosa and family also disappeared, as did the majority of the restaurant's staff. I imagine they took their bogus green cards and moved to another city to start over.

Teri was devastated by Brent's death. I think she was the only person besides his children who truly mourned him. I got her a job as a pastry apprentice at one of the hotels. Last time we talked, she had bought her first plate on the long road of replacing what Juan's henchmen had smashed.

Since there was no trial to drag Brent's name through the mud, Sharon sold American Fare at a hefty profit to some investors who would milk Brent's name for a couple of years and then sell it or close it.

Thom *had* been in the office the morning I discovered Carlos' body. He was printing up a batch of green cards when he saw the light flash on the phone console. While I was sitting in a booth crying my eyes out waiting for the cops to arrive, he walked right in front of me and out the door. I never even noticed.

In some ways, Thom benefited the most from this whole sorry affair. His father, faced with the prospect of his only son going to prison, set bail and hired him a good lawyer. His father isn't reconciled to Thom's sexuality, but at least he's back in the family fold. Thom's lawyer is trying to cut a deal with the INS. Amos keeps me posted. We're trying to figure out crimes Amos can commit so that his father will start talking to him, too.

My life began coming together slowly. I spent the first week after Brent's funeral on the couch watching videos. The next week I put my garden in order. The next month I painted the inside of my house. I bought all new furniture. I made a new quilt for my bed. I forced myself to make and eat three square meals a day and gained back all the weight I'd lost after my divorce. I discovered I still liked to cook.

The day before Thanksgiving an old teacher of mine from the École d'Epicure called and asked me if I'd be interested in a job teaching pastry. I told him yes, I'd be there after the first of the year. I had a little more than a month before the semester started, just enough time to remodel my kitchen.

One Saturday afternoon in early December, when I was poring over the blueprints for my new kitchen, the phone rang. It was O'Connor.

"How are you doing?"

I'd visualized this call many times, but now that I had the receiver in my hand I didn't know what to say.

"Good, real good. I've gained fifteen pounds. I have a new job. I start after the New Year. What about you?"

"Good. We're going to Disneyland next week with the kids. I'm trying to spend as much time with them as I can before I go back on active duty."

"Any luck tracing the wine and drug trail?"

"No." He sounded frustrated. "The department hired a computer expert to try and resurrect Juan's files, but no go, the hard drive is missing. We combed his apartment but it was squeaky clean. There weren't even bank statements. The guy must have shredded everything after the first murder. We brought in the FBI and Interpol to try to find the connection in Chile. Nada. Vino Blanco's disappeared. The Swiss won't cooperate with us. We have nothing. No paper trail, no case."

There was an awkward silence.

"Um, how are the ribs?" I asked.

"Tender, but getting better. In another month I won't even remember."

"I'm seeing a therapist next week. About Jim, the divorce. I need to work out this anger."

"He's a good guy, Mary," he reminded me.

"Yeah, I thought so at one time. Maybe I can do so again."

"Moira and I are in marriage counseling. It's helping."

Another silence.

"Mary, about that day…"

I interrupted him.

"O'Connor, I want to thank you for saving my life, then I think I need to hang up."

"Mary?"

I gripped the receiver, digging my nails into the plastic.

"We can't go there. You know that."

His voice was low and gentle. "I know. I just want to say two things. First, you're fast on your feet, gutsy, and smart. The best. All those years, I couldn't understand what Jim saw in you. Now I do. If you ever need me, call. Day or night, you understand?"

"I need to go," I said softly.

"One more thing," he insisted. "I want you to know that I'm sorry about that afternoon. Not sorry that something almost happened, sorry that something didn't happen. Good-bye, Mary."

He hung up.

I put the receiver back in the cradle.

I'd finally stopped yelling.

I picked up my blueprints. In one month I'd have one of those top-of-the-line, super-silent, German-made dishwashers to match my six-burner cooktop and double oven.

I thought, I'll make a chocolate cake in the morning. Devil's food.

Nancy Silverton has a great recipe for devil's food cake.

I could almost taste it.

To receive a free catalog of other Poisoned Pen Press titles, please contact us in one of the following ways:

Phone: 1-800-421-3976
Facsimile: 1-480-949-1707
Email: info@poisonedpenpress.com
Website: www.poisonedpenpress.com

Poisoned Pen Press
6962 E. First Ave. Ste 103
Scottsdale, AZ 85251